Hitched

Love Burns Series: Book Six

Isobel Reed

The characters and events in this book are fictitious. Any similarity to real persons, living or dead, places, or events is coincidental and not intended by the author.

If you purchase this book without a cover you should be aware that this book may have been stolen property and reported as "unsold and destroyed" to the publisher. In such case the author has not received any payment for this "stripped book."

Hitched
Love Burns Series: Book Six
Copyright © 2025 Isobel Reed
All rights reserved.

ISBN (ebook) 978-1-964636-60-3
(print) 978-1-964636-61-0

Inkspell Publishing
207 Moonglow Circle #101
Murrells Inlet, SC 29576

Edited By Toni Kelley
Cover art By Emily's World By Design

DEDICATION

For all the runaway brides scared they might be going to
hell—it could be worse, you could have settled for
someone already living down there.

ISOBEL REED

CHAPTER ONE

You're going to hell, Bethany. Straight up, Lucifer shoving pokers up your ass, hell.

"You had to go for the ball gown wedding dress, didn't you?" Bethany tutted to herself.

To be fair, at the time, she had no idea she would be trying to cram four layers of tulle out the bathroom window. In hindsight, a simple A-line would have been more suitable for this kind of thing.

Are you seriously thinking about runaway bride attire right now?

She was. Anything was better than thinking about what she was actually doing.

Finally free of the much smaller than she'd thought, bathroom window, she felt her heels sink into the freshly cut grass.

"Okay. Now what? Call an Uber?" she muttered to herself as her eyes darted around the church yard. Thank God everyone was inside. Well. Almost everyone.

Shit!

Before she'd even had a chance to gather her dress and realize that her heart was in her throat, the man in the black fitted suit was walking toward her. Their gazes locked.

Shit. Shit. Shit.

"What the hell are you doing?" the man hollered as he continued in her direction.

The nerve. He, of all people, had no right to be angry.

"You're still smoking?" was her haughty reply.

Those familiar green eyes narrowed. "What?"

"You're still smoking?" she repeated. "Don't you know those things will kill you?"

Way to pull off self-righteousness mid-way through ditching your wedding, Bethany.

"That's what you wanna talk about?" he scoffed, stopping just close enough for the sharp edge of his forest scent to wrap around her. "Not the fact that you just climbed out of that window behind you?" Benny pointed to the cloudy, rippled glass over her shoulder.

"Did you bring your truck?" she asked with a tilt of her head.

He blinked. "What?"

"Your truck, Benny, did you bring it?" She let out an exasperated sigh.

His look was beyond suspicious. "Of course, I brought my truck, B, I didn't fucking fly here."

Fucking smartass. Some things never change.

Beggars can't be choosers.

"Well, what are we waiting for? Let's go!" Her hand was in his seconds later as she hurriedly dragged him across the abandoned courtyard. Dodging uneven cobbles and century-old tree roots as she went.

Just when she didn't think this day could get more fucked up, she was gathering four layers of tulle again and cramming it into her ex-boyfriend's old pickup truck.

Fuck you too, universe.

Benny climbed in next to her, not hiding the dirty looks he was casting as he started the old banger. And it *was* an old banger. He'd been driving the faded red beast for going on thirteen years. She even remembered when he'd first gotten it, the paint was still shiny then, and you could make out the two-tone design on the bench seat fabric. Now, not so much.

Her eyes darted to the threadbare cloth, then to the

cracked dashboard as the truck rumbled to life. "Nice to know your fear of commitment doesn't extend to everything in your life," she muttered under her breath.

Benny's head snapped her way. Dark green orbs narrowing on her. "You got something you wanna say?"

"Oh, I don't know, maybe, hurry the hell up!" she impatiently huffed, her arms crossing over her chest. "If you haven't noticed, I'm kind of in a rush?"

She didn't know why she was so mad at him. Actually, scrap that. She knew. She was annoyed he was there to witness the shitshow that is her life. Pissed he'd had the audacity to show up to her wedding. And to top it all off, she was angry as hell that he still looked so damn fine.

Ten years had been kind to Benjamin Tucker. His boyish features had matured. His toned body had turned muscular. His wild chestnut hair, tamed. Even the bump in his nose he'd received after a classmate slammed open the locker door next to him, looked rugged paired with day-old stubble.

Men suck.

"I'm sorry I'm not living up to your getaway driver standards, B!" he snorted. "Maybe you want to explain to me what the fuck is going on?"

She stayed quiet. That was definitely not something she wanted to do. At least they were moving. And there were no signs of her being followed.

"Or, whereabouts I'm taking you?" he pressed.

She didn't have an answer for that, either. Running out on her wedding wasn't exactly on her list of things to do today. Right now, she was supposed to be Mrs. Douglas Wright. But she couldn't do it. Staring at her reflection in that bathroom mirror, it had hit her like a ton of bricks. Her nausea wasn't nerves. The tightness in her chest on the drive over wasn't anticipation. And the churn in her stomach certainly wasn't butterflies.

The adrenaline was waning though, which meant she had to start feeling. It's why she let her eyes flutter shut at the first sign of stinging.

"B?" Benny called out.

Hello? I'm trying not to cry here!

Hearing her first love's voice wasn't helping. It was no wonder the tears won.

"Hey?" She noticed Benny's voice gentled. "NeNe, baby, you okay?"

The use of his nickname for her, combined with a 'baby,' was enough to jolt her back to reality and quite possibly push her over the edge.

"No, I'm not okay. I just ran out on my wedding. My *freaking* wedding!" Her voice might have risen. "I have nowhere to go 'cause my parents will be pissed as hell I've run out on a wedding *they* paid for. I can't go back to my brand-new apartment 'cause the man I just left standing at the altar lives there. And if that's not enough of a shit sandwich, I'm currently sitting in a big-ass white wedding dress in a truck I not only lost my virginity in, but with the man who fucking took it—with no money, no clothes and no idea what the hell I'm going to do. So, no. I'm not o-fucking-kay."

She threw her head back, loudly sighing as it met metal. She forgot there was no headrest. *You don't deserve a headrest.* No. She didn't. She needed to prepare for discomfort before her trip to hell.

You might have already arrived.

Unsurprisingly, her rant was met with silence, which she was taking as a good thing. She didn't have any answers to his questions. She needed time, quiet, to figure out some sort of a plan.

Ten minutes of charged silence later, she let out a sigh when she still hadn't come up with one. When the truck began to slow, her attention went from the ring finger she'd been fiddling with to the front window, just in time to watch Benny pull into a cobblestone driveway.

"Where are we?" Bethany asked as she kept her gaze on the modest wood house.

Benny was already out of the truck and rounding the hood when he hollered, "Come on." Before she knew it, he'd swung open her door and was offering his hand.

"Where are we?" she repeated as she allowed him to help her out. There was too much tulle to turn him down.

"My place, NeNe. You're staying with me."

Like hell she was!

***

Bethany's white wedding dress had been mocking her, so after a quick change, she'd come back downstairs to find Benny in his kitchen. It wasn't at all what she'd expected. With butcher block counters, freshly painted duck egg cabinets and a gleaming cream backsplash, the space had a cozy country cottage feel to it. It was also spotless, as if it had been finished just yesterday.

Impressive.

Her gaze went to the half bottle of whiskey on the floating island they stood beside. A tumbler streaked with sticky amber residue signaling her ex had just downed a drink. She was tempted to pour a measure for herself. Or five.

"Are those my boxer shorts?" Her focus went back to Benny. His nostrils flaring as his gaze drifted down the length of her.

She recognized that look. And how dangerous it was. The heat in his eyes. A healthy dose of pissed off tinging the dark green, which was only getting darker as he stalked toward her.

Damnit. She shivered. Her body remembering too much.

You were about to be a married woman, Bethany. Pull yourself together.

The reminder fell on deaf ears. Benny was in her space. All too familiar warm woodsy musk making it hard to breathe.

His hand went to her shirt where he pinched the navy material sitting above her waist. "My fire department tee?" One eyebrow raised, all accusatory. "You think you're stealing this, NeNe?" That was exactly what she was doing. "Well, think again."

When she didn't reply, his grip tightened, the baggy cotton growing tighter and tighter against her skin. Not helping the whole breathing thing.

Benny's attention went to her hair next. No longer pristinely pinned, it lay loose over her shoulders. Slowly, his fingers traced the length of a messy brown strand, before sliding it between his thumb and forefinger. When he let the strand slip, and his gaze met hers again, she knew she was in trouble. Big trouble. The kind where if you don't run screaming now, you'll end up naked on your ex-boyfriend's kitchen floor regretting your life choices.

Because you're really acing the whole life choices thing today, aren't you?

"I-I," *I what? Think.* "I should go." Yes. She should. But where?

I could ask Lucy?

Lucy was the only friend she had that still lived in Woodvalley Pines. But calling her meant turning on her phone. Explaining why she'd run out on her wedding. And what on earth she was doing at her ex-boyfriend's house…in his boxer shorts. All things she wasn't quite ready to deal with just yet.

Shit.

She didn't move. Which was lucky because she didn't think she'd get very far with Benny still clinging onto her shirt.

"And where have you decided to go—to your parents or to the man you left at the altar?"

Those pathetically sad options were looking better and better by the second as more sharp ex-boyfriend fumes invaded her senses.

"I'll stay in a hotel," she rushed out, before remembering

the small town didn't exactly have a thriving tourist district. Benny's brows lifted, clearly thinking the same thing. But then her memory finally proved useful. "Oh!" she exclaimed. "The Evans brothers!" She was gleefully pointing her finger in his direction now. "They opened guest cabins a while back, I'll go stay there!"

Benny's face hardened. "No."

"No?" she repeated. Unsure what that look on his face was all about.

"No," he said again. "You'll stay here. I'll have Rachel go get your things from your apartment."

Who the hell was Rachel? *Oh. Is that his girlfriend?*

Just the thought had Bethany stepping back. Releasing her shirt from Benny's hold and breaking the spell his eyes had her under.

Her gaze dropped to the floor, suddenly finding the shiny wood beams far more interesting than him. But it didn't last long, Benny's black loafers stepped back into her space, and a moment later, his big hand was cradling her cheek, gently tipping her head up to meet him.

"She's my friend's wife." God, she hated that he knew exactly what she was thinking. And how darn smug that grin was. "She's also too damn nice to turn away so she'll have no problem getting your things."

Nice or not, she had a feeling Doug wasn't going to just let some stranger waltz into his home and take her stuff.

"That's nice of you, but it's not necessary. I'll grab some bits from the Farm n' Fresh on my way over to the Evans ranch."

Are you seriously gonna walk around the Farm n' Fresh in Benny's boxers?

Her inner voice made a good point. She'd caused enough scandal for one day. This town was far too small. Back in Denver she never had to worry about small town gossip. She remembered then, more shit to add to the show. She'd just moved her residency to the Goldacre Medical Clinic.

Just freaking peachy.

11

"What was that look?" The concern in Benny's voice snapped her back to reality.

"Nothing," she lied. "Can I borrow some sweats?"

He took a moment to run his eyes up and down her again. Heat scorching her skin as he did. When he was done, instead of answering her question, he pulled out his phone.

"Yeah," he grunted in reply to the mystery person on the other end of his call. "I need a favor." She resisted the urge to impatiently tap her foot as another second passed. "I need you and Rachel to pass by Bethany's apartment and gather some clothes and shit and bring them here."

Really?

The man was infuriating.

"Yeah. I'll text you the address."

This is how murders happen.

CHAPTER TWO

It was safe to say, this was not exactly how Benny thought this day was going to go. His plan was to go to the ceremony. Witness Bethany getting married. Leave. Then celebrate his newfound closure with alcohol. That obviously didn't happen. And his ex, standing before him in nothing but his shirt and boxers clearly wasn't closure. It was the exact fucking opposite of that shit.

"Did you hear me?" Bethany impatiently called out. Her arms crossing over her chest as angry jade eyes narrowed on him. "I'm not staying with you, Benny. Just give me some sweats and drop me off at the Evans ranch."

That wasn't happening. He knew Bethany. Better than anyone. Right now, she needed quiet. Time to clear her head. Make a plan. As nice as the Evans ranch was, it was a small fricking town, and he'd give it an hour before her parents and a disgruntled ex-fiancé would be knocking down her door.

Unfortunately, he also knew how stubborn she was.

"You really wanna do this, B? Spend the next hour making a pros and cons list?" The daggers she was giving him momentarily faltered. That was enough for him to know her stubborn was penetrable. So, he continued. "'Cause, I'll do it if I have to. I'll tell you all the reasons staying at the Evans ranch isn't really what you *want* or *need*.

I don't know about you, but I'm tired as hell, and I'd rather just skip to the part where you give me the address."

All right, so he wasn't tired, per se. But the head fuck that was Bethany Mayer was definitely making it hard to think clearly. Especially standing there in his kitchen looking like a goddamn wet dream.

It might have been almost a decade since they'd last seen each other but his body remembered her all too well. And it was begging him to do something about the fire shooting through his veins.

That wasn't going to happen. He'd sooner let his body burn than risk his heart shattering again. He'd been picking up the pieces ever since Bethany walked away ten years ago, and he wasn't about to start over.

"And you're such an expert on my *wants* and *needs*, right Benny?"

Don't even think about it.

Benny ignored the warning, his body humming in response, vividly recalling every dirty little thing his ex-girlfriend liked.

Stop.

"Wipe that look off your face!" she scolded, mortified. "You don't get to do that anymore."

He felt his lips twitch as he fought back a smile. "I don't get to do *what* anymore?" he asked, happily pushing his luck.

Bethany stomped her foot while her bright eyes flashed. "You know *what!*"

The pink tinging her cheeks told a very different story to the scowl she was trying to muster. And was enough to propel him forward, back in her space, his fingers instinctively going to her hair again, this time to tuck a loose wave behind her ear.

"Looks like I'm not the only one taking a trip down memory lane, NeNe," he muttered, letting the pad of his thumb slowly glide across her heated cheek. "One of the perks of being someone's ex is that no matter what happens—the shit I got stored up here—is mine." He made a point of tapping his index finger to his head. *"All fucking mine."*

Pink turned to red as Bethany's breathing hitched. It was safe to say, she hadn't forgotten any more than he had. Should he be concerned at how pleased that made him?

Um. Yes!

Bethany took a whole step back. Then another. And then one more. Giving her time to rearrange her facial expression from hot and heavy to cold and indifferent.

Before she put him in his place though, his phone pinged, bringing both their attention to the device he began sliding out of his pocket. Swiping on his friend Hunter's name, relief flooded him as he read the message.

Thank God for that.

He really didn't have the emotional energy to fight. He wasn't in much of a fit state for anything if he was being honest. Even after the first cigarette he'd smoked in years at the church and an overly generous pour of whiskey once he got home, his heart was still pounding like it was trying to break free.

"Hunter and Rachel will be over in a little while with your stuff," he rasped. "They got the address from Mrs. Molly and are heading over there now."

He watched on as confusion, anger, annoyance, and then some more anger washed over her delicate features. Bringing back even more memories.

He bit back a smirk as a frustrated growl echoed around the small kitchen.

"Unbelievable," she huffed as she spun around and went straight to his fridge. "Fuck my fucking life," she went on as she pulled out not one, not two, but three cans of his beer before swaying her perfect ass out of there.

"By all means, help yourself, B," he shouted after her.

Resting a hip against the kitchen island, he smiled. A huge grin that was bigger than it should be. He'd allow it for now. Treat himself to five minutes of happy. There was plenty of time to panic. Question what the fuck he'd just done. And then worry about the ache in his chest and the knots in his stomach.

***

"You sure you know what you're doing?"

Hunter's question wasn't surprising. Especially since Benny didn't, in fact, know what the fuck he was doing. Something he suspected his friend was well aware of as he passed him another suitcase.

Not ready to admit that yet though, Benny changed the subject. "Jesus, man. You got her fucking couch in there, too? Why'd you bring so much stuff?"

"Three suitcases is not a lot of stuff, sugar," Rachel chirped, rejoining them on the porch. "Right." His fiery-haired friend aimed her finger at him, demanding his attention. "I put the lasagna in the fridge, a few ready meals in the freezer, and the muffins on the counter. Oh, and there's a double chocolate and peanut butter sponge in the tin next to the microwave."

Benny's gaze went from Rachel to Hunter and then back to Rachel. "Am I missing something …what's with all the food? Did someone die?"

Hunter remained silent but when Benny looked back, he didn't miss the goofy grin the six- foot-five hulk had pasted across his face, which only got bigger as his wife began to speak.

"Yes. *Love* died, Benny. It died a horrible death." He stood silent as she planted her hands on her hips. "And that poor girl in there is gonna need pasta and chocolate, so you make sure you look after her."

Benny loved Rachel, but she was dramatic as hell.

"You know that *that poor girl*, is the one who left some dude at the altar, right?"

If anything, Doug was the one who could do with some carbs and sugar. He kept that particular thought to himself, though. Rachel may be small, but she was also pretty scary

when she wanted to be. He knew better than to anger her.

Proving his point, Rachel gave him an incredulous look. "She was going to marry that man, Benny. What's wrong with you?" *Me?* "She must be absolutely heartbroken. A break-up is a break-up, no matter who left who. You just be nice." Another finger was jabbed in his face. "And give her the cake. Libby, Bella, Cat and I are all here if she needs to talk to someone who doesn't have the emotional intelligence of a twelve-year-old."

Hunter guffawed as Benny shot him a dirty look.

Libby was married to Zach, while Bella was Luke's girlfriend. Zach, Luke and Hunter all worked together as firefighters for the Woodvalley Fire Department. And Cat was married to Cody, the local police deputy. They'd all been friends for years and now the women were part of that friend group, too.

"Uh. Hey." Benny, Rachel and Hunter's attention all went to the coy voice behind them. Bethany. She was still in his fire department shirt, and boxers. Looking like a goddamn goddess as her fingers drifted over the suitcase Benny was still holding. "Wow. I can't believe Doug let you take all this stuff."

Rachel was the one to reply, unsurprisingly. "He's...he asked me to give you this." A note was pulled from his friend's jean pocket and handed to Bethany. "I'm Rachel, by the way."

Benny's eyes stayed glued to the note. He hated that he wanted to know what it said. Really badly. He wanted to know if Bethany would read it. And if she did, would the words in there make her change her mind. Would she take her three suitcases and go back to this Doug guy? Leaving Benny. Again.

What the fucking, fuck?

His inner voice wasn't exactly thrilled with the choices he'd been making today. Now it was pissed with his thought process, too.

Perfect.

He faintly heard Bethany introduce herself and thank Rachel and Hunter for collecting her things as she twiddled the folded piece of paper between her fingers. But it was only when he heard her say, "I feel so bad, but I can't. I'm not ready," that his eyes went to her face. Her usual light dulling as her gaze hit the ground.

His hand instinctively shot out and curled around Bethany's waist as he pulled her into him.

"Hey," he waited until her head lifted, and shimmering eyes locked onto his before continuing. "It's gonna be okay. You did the right thing, B." He ignored the feeling of his friend's eyes burning into the back of his head. "I don't know about Doug, but I sure as hell wouldn't want to marry someone who was having second thoughts on the wedding day. You both deserve more. You deserve to know, NeNe, that you're marrying your soulmate." As her gaze softened, he had to take a second to gulp. "Forever should mean *forever*."

He noticed Bethany swallow just as hard as she released herself from his hold. But when she opened her plump lips to say something, she was quick to slam them shut before anything had the chance to come out. Leaving Benny's mind to race as she offered him nothing more than a single nod before practically running back inside the house.

Letting a sigh slip, he turned back to his friends, both of whom had stupid smiles on their faces.

"What?" he asked impatiently.

Hunter simply shook his head, his large smirk openly mocking Benny.

"I never thought I'd see the day," Rachel oddly replied.

Benny repeated his question and was met with more words that didn't make any sense.

"Wait until I tell the girls." Rachel giggled.

Tell the girls what?

More sighing ensued as Benny came to the decision that he'd rather not know. Today had already been way more than he'd bargained for and it was nowhere near over.

After saying his goodbyes and thanking his friends for their help, he headed upstairs in search of Bethany. He was under strict instructions to make sure she knew there was pasta and chocolate waiting for her.

She'd gone straight to his bedroom again. Was it weird that was where she was most comfortable? Not the living room. The kitchen. Or the guest bedroom. *His* room. Yes, it made sense to change her clothes in there earlier so she could raid his wardrobe, but she'd gone back. First with three of his beers after their exchange in the kitchen, and now after hightailing it off the porch.

One knock on the door and he was allowed entry, but he wasn't quite prepared for what he found when he took a step inside. Bethany on his bed. Wearing his clothes. Wrapped up in his sheets. Silky dark waves splayed over his pillow.

Fuck me.

His throat tightened. It had been a long damn time since he'd been treated to this particular sight.

"I, I, uh," Jesus, he was pathetic. "There's food. Rachel brought food."

Bethany's head came up and he didn't miss her red rimmed eyes. She'd been crying. Damnit. Every instinct he had screamed at him to go to her. Pull her into his arms. Tell her everything was going to be okay. But he couldn't. He didn't trust himself. So, he stayed rooted to his spot by the doorframe, willing his body to calm the hell down and his head to clear.

It's not working.

It wasn't. Not when she began to chew on her lips. Her chest heaving as she looked at him with soft hooded eyes. It was taking all the willpower he had to not march over there and replace her teeth with his mouth.

What the hell is wrong with you?

He had no fucking idea. It didn't matter that she was his ex, that he hadn't seen her since she was nineteen. The fact that just a few hours ago, she'd been moments away from marrying someone else should have been enough to snap him out of it.

"Thank you," her voice was uncharacteristically quiet.

"Rachel made it—"

"No," she cut him off. "Thank *you*, Benny." He must have looked confused because she decided to elaborate. "For everything. The lift. A place to stay. Getting my stuff. I appreciate it."

He didn't know what to say. Sassy, fiery Bethany he could handle. But sweet, vulnerable Bethany, her voice trembling, her eyes sad—there was no way he stood a chance.

Get the hell out of there.

Lucky for him, the next words she spoke gave him an out. "I think I'm just gonna stay up here with my beer if that's okay?"

Still clearly unable to string a sentence together, he decided to give her a nod before quickly backing out of the room.

Coward!

There was no point in denying it. When it came to Bethany Mayer, there was no denying it. He was the coward of all cowards.

CHAPTER THREE

This morning, Bethany should have been waking up to the view of Cabo's white sandy beaches. She should have been in her private pool, soaking up the sun and quite possibly a large Margarita while nibbling on the elaborate breakfast delivered to the honeymoon suite. She should have been married. And happy.

But thanks to the dumpster fire that was her life, where was she waking up instead? Her ex-boyfriend's bedroom, that's where. Wrapped in pine-scented sheets, that she couldn't quite stop herself from drinking in all night.

I hate myself.

A sentiment she voiced by moaning into the soft feather pillow before forcing herself onto her back. There, she stared at the wooden beams above her, wondering when the hell Benjamin Tucker grew up. This was the room of an actual adult male. There were no peeling posters of dirt bikes and rock bands. Clothes weren't scattered everywhere and the only things cluttering the nightstand were the three empty cans of beer she'd drowned her sorrows with last night.

Right. Hence the pounding in my head.

Or was it her chest that was still thumping so hard it was likely shaking the rest of her body, too? Her eyes went to that note again, positioned between two cans. *Fuck.* There was so much she had to do. Speak to Doug, to her parents, figure out what to do with the apartment, where she was going to live.

Maybe start by turning on your phone?

She really didn't want to do that. Doug's note was bad enough; she wasn't mentally prepared for her inbox yet.

Talking of things she wasn't ready to face, her head shot up as two knocks hit the bedroom door.

"B?" Benny called before knocking once more. "I made you some coffee."

Coffee sounded great. Seeing her first love again while she had smudged make-up, bad breath and hair that looked like she'd just been electrocuted, did not.

"I'll be down in a sec!" she called out, hoping he'd get the hint.

Last night, once his friends had left, Benny had left her alone with her beers, only knocking once to let her know her bags were by the door. She appreciated the time alone. She needed it. But now it was time to face the music.

"You sure, I brought it up so you can have it in bed?"

Of course he did. He knew she liked her coffee in bed before she even thought about getting up and ready for the day. But as much as she wanted coffee in bed, she wanted her dignity more. Which was why she declined and braved leaving the bed in search of a bathroom. Another good sized, adult room just next to the bedroom, with a fancy whitewashed brick wall behind the vanity and her dream walk-in shower with black metal framing around the glass.

Is he an interior designer now or what?

Seeing just how put together her ex's life was, really wasn't helping her feel less like shit. He'd clearly done well for himself. And he seemed happy.

Without me.

Yes. Without her. Not that she expected him to have spent the last decade pining after her. That was highly unlikely, not just because of who he was, but that sort of thing doesn't tend to happen to the person who made the decision to end things. All that fun stuff was left for the dumpee. Her.

Okay. Time to wash her dumped ass and sort her life out.

***

Feeling slightly less like a hot mess, Bethany was back in the kitchen twenty minutes later, this time in her own clothes. She'd thrown on some jeans and a black tank and let her hair dry naturally around her shoulders.

With a fresh mug of coffee in her hand, she was in the middle of eyeing some extremely tempting muffins when Benny's voice boomed from the doorway.

"Lemon curd poppy seed." She looked up to find him casually slumped against the doorframe, "and yes, they're for you."

"For me?" Bethany's head tilted suspiciously with the question.

"Yup." Benny straightened, and she couldn't help but admire the view as he swaggered over. He was freshly showered too, the tips of his hair still damp. She didn't know what she liked more, the navy fire department T-shirt on him or her. Or maybe it was the waft of freshly sprayed cologne tickling her tongue. "Rachel owns a bakery in town, she thought you might like them."

She thought right.

Plucking one of the soft, golden treats from the linen, Benny held it out for her, a knowing glint in his eyes as if daring her to resist.

As she reached for the muffin, her fingers brushed against his, sending a spark she wasn't quite prepared for, shooting all the way up her arm. Rendering her frozen. Instead of pulling away though, Benny's touch lingered. His eyes never leaving hers as his fingertips grazed her palm. Softly. Deliberately. Enough to make her breath hitch until she finally remembered to pull back.

She'd never been very good at resisting. Especially when

it came to Benjamin Tucker.

Would you please stop. You've been single eighteen freaking hours. And he's your fucking ex!

Only he wasn't just an ex. That was the problem when it came to Benny. She wished he was just some guy she dated for a few months, even a year. But he wasn't. He was her first everything and always would be. Her first love, her first kiss, her first time. But more importantly, the first and only person to break her heart. We're talking shattering here. Like, some of the pieces that broke off were so small she still isn't completely sure where the bits went. Or if they would ever be found again.

Shouldn't you be feeling that now...after ending things with Doug? You know, the man you were supposed to marry!

She didn't want to think about why she didn't. Or the volumes that spoke. She was way too embarrassed for that.

"NeNe? Did you hear me?"

She must have spaced out because she had definitely not heard him.

"Huh?"

An easy smile tugged at his lips. "You gonna eat that muffin or challenge it to a dual?"

"A *dual?*" She didn't hide the amusement in her voice. "Actually, I was thinking more like pistols at dawn."

A deep throaty laugh echoed around the small space, sending more tingles to more places that definitely shouldn't be tingling.

She'd take tingly over hard to breathe any day though, which is what she was treated with next. When the laughter stopped, his dark eyes locked onto hers. And got darker, until all she saw was black as Benny drifted closer. Close enough for her to become intoxicated all over again, her nostrils most likely flaring as she unashamedly inhaled him. Her eyelids fluttering closed as she got higher and higher on his scent.

She kept her eyes tightly shut as stubble scraped her chin. She should be worried about how easily her body succumbed to this man. How quickly her mind malfunctions when he's close. That worry was nowhere to be found as her lips parted for him, ready and eager to swallow the feral growl he just let slip.

But his taste never tinged her tongue, because a moment later, angry, loud bangs tore them apart. It took a minute for her brain to restart and when it did, Benny was already stalking toward the front door.

Oh, God. Angry knocking. Bethany doubted Benny had pissed anyone off in the past twenty-four hours. Which meant only one thing. Someone had found her. Either Doug or her parents. As she cursed her way out of the kitchen, she had no idea which she preferred.

One look at Doug's red face though, and she started to regret getting her ass over there quite so quickly.

"*Him*, Bethany. *Him!*" Venom spiked the words as Doug waved his finger in Benny's direction while his rage-soaked stare pinned her in place. "You spent the night with *him!*"

Oh boy. He was so angry. His usually handsome profile looking almost deranged with wild brown hair and even wilder eyes coming at her.

"Hey!" Benny jumped in, "lower your voice, man."

He did not lower his voice, if anything, it got louder. "I knew it! I knew you weren't over him. The infamous *Ben fucking Tucker*." She shivered at the icy edge in his voice. "But to do *this*—*on our wedding night*. I feel sick. *You're* fucking sick."

"Nothing—" She wanted to explain, but he cut her off.

"Shut the fuck up!"

"Hey!" Benny took a step forward, pushing Bethany behind him as he got in Doug's face. "Watch your goddamn mouth."

Peeking over Benny's shoulder, her gaze followed as Doug's eyes cut to Benny, his expression barely masking the disgust he had for him. "Three fucking years she wasted. Well, I hope you enjoy fixing what you broke, *Loverboy*. I'm done playing cleanup." What was she supposed to say to that? What was Benny? "You can have the bitch."

Ummm. Unnecessary!

That, she had a reply to, unfortunately she wasn't able to get it out before Benny had his hands on Doug's collar as he hurled him up close and spoke into him.

"Listen up and listen good. The only reason my fist isn't rearranging your face right now is because you got left at the altar yesterday. Consider this your one and only free pass. But from now on, you stay the fuck away from Bethany. You don't look at her. You don't speak to her. And you sure as hell don't raise your voice at her. Are we clear?"

Damn. That was way better than what she was going to say. And really hot.

Doug wriggled free from Benny's grip, no less angry. But the lack of venom being hurled her way indicated he did indeed understand.

Guilt twisted her stomach. This was all her fault. She'd been a coward. First by running away, then by switching off her phone. The realization propelled her forward. Made her do what she should have done yesterday. Speak.

"I'm so sorry, Doug. Nothing happened with Benny, I swear on my life." Her hand went to his arm but was quickly shaken off. "I shouldn't have run. I should have stayed and talked to you. You deserved a conversation, I know that. If I could go back, *take it all back*, I would. I would've done things differently." She paused to take a breath. "I'm truly sorry. The last thing I ever wanted to do was hurt you."

When she was done, one look at Doug told her that he wasn't in any rush to forgive and forget anytime soon, which was fair.

His parting "fuck you" still stung though.

Benny was ready to pounce as Doug turned, but her hand shot out. Stopping him in his tracks. "Leave it," she whispered. "It's done. It's over."

Even as she said the words, she didn't believe them. Nothing was over, if anything, it had only just begun.

CHAPTER FOUR

Benny's knee was bouncing again, his gaze going back to his phone screen. It had been four whole days since Bethany Mayer had come crashing back into his life, and three whole days since she packed up her shit and disappeared again.

After her not so friendly ex banged down his door, she couldn't get out of there quick enough. Benny hadn't even had a chance to get her new number before she was cramming everything into a cab and shouting out her thank yous and goodbyes. He didn't even know if she was still in town. And if she was, whether she was sticking around or moving back to Denver.

"You ready to talk about it yet?" his friend Zach asked as he bounced down on the raggedy couch next to him.

No.

Benny was back on shift at the fire station. And his friends apparently wanted answers.

"I know where she's staying," Zach added, knowing full well that would get Benny's attention.

"The ranch?" he was quick to ask. Zach and his brothers owned the Evans ranch, so if anyone was going to know if she checked in, he would.

"Nope, word is, she went straight from yours to Lucy's."

What? "Lucy? From the diner?"

Zach nodded in confirmation as Benny tried his hardest

to think back. Yes, Lucy had been in the same year as them in school, but he didn't recall Bethany being anything more than acquaintances with her. Not that there was anything wrong with Lucy, she was sweet and everything, but she was on the shy side which was the complete opposite of his NeNe.

Your NeNe?

Damnit. He was doing it again. Ever since their almost kiss, his brain kept conveniently forgetting Bethany wasn't his anything anymore.

"So?" Zach prompted. "You gonna tell me what's going on? How it just so happened the only woman you've ever loved ran out on her wedding day—and ended up back at your place?"

The only woman you've ever loved. Ouch.

It was the truth, but still, those words stung like a motherfucker.

"There's nothing to tell."

"Really?" Zach wasn't exactly convinced. "Is that why you're sitting here with a face like a slapped ass?"

"A face like a *slapped ass*?" Benny finally managed to crack a smile while he shook his head in disbelief at his friend. "Man, you spend way too much time with Cat."

Zach simply chuckled, not even attempting to deny he'd stolen that line from his wife's British best friend.

"Who's got a face like a slapped ass?" Luke snuck up from behind them, quickly planting himself on the creaky wooden chair next to the couch.

"Who'd ya think?" Zach grinned. "He says *there's nothing to tell*, despite his ex spending her wedding night in *his* bed."

"*He's* sitting right here." Benny moaned. This was the problem with small towns and nosy-ass friends.

Never one to miss an opportunity to give him a hard time, Luke decided to pipe up next. "According to Hunter, you were waxing all poetic to her. Talking about soulmates and some shit." *What the actual fuck?* "Dude!" Luke called out to the big man in question, who just so happened to be close by in the staff kitchen. "What was it you said Benny was calling his ex when you went over—Nona?"

Kill me now.

Next thing he knew, Hunter was pulling up a rickety chair. "NeNe," he grunted, a small smile tugging his traitorous lips as he offered Benny a chin lift.

He could shove his chin lift.

"Right." Luke laughed. *Bastard.* "You two hook-up?"

Benny shot him a glare.

"Is that a, yes?" His friend's dark brow raised with the question.

"I think it's more of a *go fuck yourself*," Zach gleefully chirped. His signature dimples on full display.

Luke's smile widened, too. "I've got to hand it to you, man—convincing a woman to bail on her *own wedding* is a whole new level of fuckboy behavior."

Benny rolled his eyes at that. "I didn't convince Bethany to do anything, you asshole. She needed a lift and a place to crash. That's it. End of story. Now, if you don't mind, some of us have work to do."

Benny rose from his seat despite having no work to do. They were between callouts, the trucks were clean, checks were complete, and their next training drill wasn't until next week. But he needed an out. Fast.

"A lift? A place to crash? That's the story you're sticking with?" Luke replied. All three men were now snickering. "'Cause you should know... half the town thinks she left that man at the altar because she's never gotten over you, and the other half thinks you stormed the church and practically *kidnapped* her because you never got over her."

"For the love of God." Benny's hand went behind his neck where his fingers dug into newly tightened muscles.

"You know, if you wanted to tell us what's actually going on..." Zach started, "then as your loyal friends, we could set the record straight for you."

With not much of a choice, Benny's ass fell back into the weathered couch cushions. As much as he didn't want to talk about Bethany, ever, he also didn't want the likes of Mrs. Molly and Betsy-Jane banging down his door, either.

"Fine," he said through gritted teeth. "I ran into her in the church yard, making a break for it. She needed a ride, so I gave her one. She was upset and freaking out and she had nowhere to go 'cause everyone was gonna be pissed at her, so I took her to my place. It was the only option."

"The only option?" Hunter had officially joined the conversation.

Benny nodded. It *was* the only option. Bethany hadn't lived in Woodvalley Pines in ten years, any high school friends she'd had had moved away, that left her parents, the guy she just ditched at the altar and him.

And Lucy.

Fine. Lucy too, apparently. But for some reason, she hadn't wanted to call her at the time.

"You know I run a ranch with guest cabins, right?" Zach unnecessarily reminded him.

"I think what he's trying to say is...there *were* other options." Luke leaned forward, an unusually serious expression hardening his face.

With all eyes on him, Benny suddenly felt pressured. "What do you want me to say?"

"Look man," Zach's dimples were gone. Instead, his brow was furrowed, and his blue eyes were pinning Benny with another serious stare. "You joined the team not long after you guys broke up. So, *we know* how hard you took it. We were also with you when you got that invite to her wedding."

"Your point?" Benny was growing more and more impatient by the second.

"His point," Hunter interrupted, "is that it's okay to feel some kind of way. You loved her. You took the break-up hard. Now she's back in town and suddenly single."

Benny was standing again, completely over this conversation. "If you guys think for one second, I'm trying to get back with Bethany Mayer, you couldn't be more fucking wrong." His voice came out much louder than he intended but it was too late, and he was too angry to do anything about it. "In case you've forgotten, I don't do relationships. You think I'm gonna start now—with messy shit like this? Just 'cause you fuckers are off playing house, doesn't mean I want that, too."

Screw this. He was going to the bunks. He needed to calm the hell down. Alone. And maybe figure out why his palms were sweating, and why the hell his heart was beating so damn fast.

Don't forget to also figure out why all you want to do right now is drive on over to Lucy's so you can get another look at Bethany's beautiful goddamn face.

Yes. He'll get on that, too.

***

"Ma!" Benny hollered as the front door swung open. As usual, he battled through at least twenty pairs of shoes to reach the staircase, where he called out again. "Ma, you left the door open!"

"In here!" His mother's muffled words came from the kitchen. Located at the back of the house, behind the stairs, he was met with more abandoned shoes as he made his way there.

"You left the door open again," he repeated, stepping into the cheery yellow kitchen, overflowing with knick-knacks and inspirational wooden signs. Amid the chaos, his petite, white-haired mother bustled around, trying to craft cookies in the sliver of counter space left. He sighed, casting a glance back toward the front door. "Anyone could walk in, Ma. Please lock it."

Bright eyes locked onto him as she lifted her head, her familiar smile quickly spreading. "I knew you were coming over, so I opened it." She shrugged. "Saves you time fumbling with all those keys you have."

Benny scoffed. He had exactly three keys, one for his

house, one for his parents', and one for his car. Hardly enough to qualify as a janitor. But this was classic Mom, always looking for the smallest ways to make his life easier, whether he needed it or not.

Rounding the counter, his arm snaked around her shoulders as he placed a kiss on her head. "What ya making?"

After offering up his assistance, his mother went from talking cookies to launching into a full report on Auntie Jane's neighbor's son. More classic Mom. Never one to turn down a good story, Benny settled in to hear all about Mark. A man who apparently, he met once, though he had no memory of it. He went on to hear all about how Mark went from a big job in the city to living in his parents' basement. Poor guy. The best part of the story was how Auntie Jane had spotted him on a dating app. Benny had so many questions. The first being, what on earth was his *very married* auntie doing on a dating app. Followed closely by what the hell kind of profile settings did she have on that app that she was being matched with thirty-year old men?

Sometimes it's better not to know.

True. He did need to be able to sleep at night.

"Talking of people who are new in town." His mother shot him a quick glance before turning her attention to the oven. "Are we going to talk about Bethany Mayer being back…and any of the *many stories* I've heard about her wedding day?"

Jesus. Benny dragged a hand down his face. *"Many stories?"*

So much for the two versions his friends recounted yesterday.

"Yes, Benjamin. *Many.*" His mother tried for a stern glare as she placed the cookie tray on the counter but didn't quite pull it off. "Is it too much to ask that you give your mother a heads up before you storm the local church, declare your love for the bride and carry her off into the sunset?"

He couldn't stop his eyes rolling if his life depended on it. "I think you know I didn't storm the church, Ma, or do any of the unhinged things the town gossips are claiming I did."

His mom's eyebrow raised. "So, Bethany Mayer *didn't* spend her wedding night at your house?"

Shit.

Okay. So, he was guilty of one unhinged action.

Just one?

Benny was starting to miss the days when his head didn't talk back. No mocking. Commentating. Critiquing. Just quiet. Pure, beautiful, silence.

"Benjamin?"

"Yeah, uh," he coughed, "I guess that part is kinda true."

"Kinda?" He could tell his mother was trying not to smile. "So, are you going to tell me what happened of your own free will, or do I have to bribe you with cookies?"

He'd take the cookies. If he was going to admit what a dumbass he was out loud. To his mother. Then he needed compensation.

CHAPTER FIVE

"What are you doing here?" Bethany croaked, her throat all of a sudden becoming very dry.

It had been exactly one week since she'd run out of her wedding, and her life had been flipped completely upside down.

As expected, there were consequences to ending her relationship with Doug. As well as being the new social pariah of Woodvalley Pines, she'd also pissed her parents off with, to quote her mom, "her dramatic behavior," that they were avoiding her. But that was just the start, to add to the crap pile that was her life—she also no longer had a place to live as their apartment was in Doug's name. It was too late to transfer her residency back to Denver. And to top it all off, she had the total of one friend in town, Lucy, whose couch she was currently crashing on.

"B?"

Oh yeah. Then there's Benny. Your stupidly attractive ex-boyfriend who you almost kissed last week and who is now on your doorstep, looking like a rugged Greek God and expecting you to communicate by using actual words.

"Um." Water, she needed water. "What?"

"I said..." Benny eyed her suspiciously. Thank God he couldn't read minds. "I came to see how you were doing. Can I come in...I brought coffee, your favorite?" He offered her one of the steaming takeaway cups he was holding. "Caramel macchiato with whipped cream."

Well, there was a beverage on offer. A delicious one. And she was desperately close to dehydration.

Nope! Get his ass out of there, you've got enough problems.

Her Judas hand shot out to accept the drink before her brain could do something sensible for once and turn him away.

Damnit.

Resigned to her fate, she turned, her body shifting to grant him entry into Lucy's apartment. Before she followed him inside, however, she took a sip of caramel courage.

You've got this. Just don't kiss him.

History had proven that was easier said than done.

"So, you're staying with Lucy, huh? I didn't even know you guys were friends." Benny scanned the small living room. Bethany's current bedroom.

Of course, he didn't know. They weren't dumb teenagers anymore; she had a whole life he knew nothing about.

"Yeah, well, we are. And she's been kind enough to take me in until I…" *get my shit together? Sort out my life?* "Until I…find a place."

"That means you're staying?" A panty-melting smile began to tilt his lips.

Why did that smile give her such a rush? He was happy she was staying. Why was he happy?

Strategically ignoring the many questions now forming an orderly queue in her head, she went on to explain about her residency. To her surprise, Benny listened intently. Genuinely excited to hear she wanted to use her medical degree to go into family practice.

"You can set up shop in Woodvalley."

"What?"

"Woodvalley Pines. Folks here have to drive on out to Goldacre to see the doctor, but when you're done with your residency you could set up your own practice, here in town. It'd be life changing, NeNe, for everyone."

Bethany had had enough life-changing moments this week. She didn't even know if she wanted to stay in Woodvalley. Not anymore. Granted she hadn't been back long, only moving into their apartment one week before the wedding, but the reason why she returned no longer seemed valid.

Doug wanted to start a family, eventually. She'd not been especially keen but if she were ever to have kids, she always envisioned doing it in her hometown. Hence the move. But now here she was—minus one husband, homeless, and stuck.

"I don't…I'm not sure." Bethany stumbled over to the L-shaped couch and dropped down. "I haven't thought that far ahead." Actually, she had, a local practice would be exactly what she wanted for her future. But plans change. Weddings get ditched and ex-boyfriends resurface.

Luckily, there was still some caramel coffee left to comfort her, which she went on to down.

Benny joined her on the cream cushions, taking a sip of his own coffee as he studied her a bit too hard.

"There must have been a reason you moved back here in the first place, right?"

Not about to discuss her biological clock with him, she swiftly changed the subject. "How's your mom?"

"My mom's fine. So's my dad. Now, are you gonna change the subject again or you gonna tell me why you came back?"

Urgh.

"Because there *has* to be a reason?" she snarked. "What about it being my home, y'know, the place I was born, the place I grew up, where my parents live—that's not enough?"

Benny's head shook as he let out a humorless laugh. "Right, B. Although, I don't seem to recall that being enough to keep you here in the first place, was it? In fact, I remember you not being able to get out of here quick enough."

Ow. She felt that swipe right in the gut. And she didn't

miss the bitter edge he'd coated each word with.

How fricking rude. She was the dumpee, not him. Her words should be the ones coated in bitter. Not his.

"Are you really going to go there?" Bethany's spine snapped straight as she slammed her empty cup onto the coffee table.

Gone were all traces of humor on Benny's face as he also sat up a little bit straighter. "And where exactly am I going, B?"

He totally knew where.

"If you think for one second, I'm gonna let you spin our break-up into something it most definitely wasn't, you're sorely fucking mistaken." Pushing up off the cushions, she began to pace. Anger hit her hard. And really frigging fast.

Talk about triggering.

"Oh really." Benny followed suit and rose, too. "So, you're telling me you didn't leave town...without saying goodbye?" He didn't wait for her to answer before he continued. "Or change your number? And you certainly didn't ask your parents to make sure I didn't get your new address? Oh, and let's not forget how you didn't step foot in this town again for *ten fucking years*...not for birthdays or holidays or your parent's goddamn anniversary! Nothing."

Benny's voice might have been rising but Bethany could barely hear it over the pounding in her ears. It propelled her forward, into his space, where she could poke his shoulder, sharply. And then prod it again.

"Don't you dare! You're not the injured party here, I am. *I was.* I get to be mad, not you. I get to change my number and avoid you. *Me.* That's mine. That's what happens when you break a girl's heart. *She* gets to move on, and you don't get a say on where or how she does it."

Benny's eyes narrowed as her finger assaulted his shoulder once more. "Are you trying to tell me my heart didn't break too, B? Because I'm damn fucking sure it did. And I get to feel it, too. I get to be mad that you left. That you refused to speak to me. That you broke my goddamn heart and left me to bleed out."

It was getting hard to breathe. Every word felt like a blow. She tried desperately to think back. To remember how everything went down. She'd spent so long trying not to think about it, she struggled. But when the memories resurfaced, the pain was still as raw as it was then.

"No!" she shouted, her voice shaking. "*You* broke up with *me*! *You* changed your mind! *You* chose to stay here! And—" she let out a bitter laugh. "I believe your exact words were, *I have to let you go.*"

Benny took a step forward, his head dipping until his breath was close enough to hit her lips. "Even if it breaks me," he ground out, making her chest squeeze. "That's what I said, NeNe. I have to let you go, *even if it breaks me*. And make no mistake...*it did* break me."

Why is it so damn hard to breathe?

Oxygen not making it to her brain was the only excuse she had for leaning into him. Or perhaps she was bleeding out, too. The old and badly stitched wound he'd left her with was starting to split. Leaving her raw and exposed.

A slight lift of her chin left her gazing into deep green. She didn't know what she expected to see, but it wasn't the unguarded pain she found. As uneven breaths sunk into her skin, neither of them moved. The air charged with every unsaid word. Just when she thought she couldn't take anymore, callused fingertips grazed her jaw. Seeking permission.

Fuck.

Yes. Fuck. That was the last thought she had before she traced the tip of her nose against his. With the slightest tilt of her head, she closed what little distance was left between them, her lips parting as her mouth met his.

His hand pushed into her hair, as the soft brush of their lips skipped hesitant and went straight to frantic. Benny kissed her like he owned her. There was no teasing, no testing. He knew what he wanted, and he was taking it. Every tongue swipe took him deeper, his grip on her hair only growing tighter as he feasted on her whimpers.

His big body moved her backward until she found herself up against the wall. The last of her control snapping as he pressed his full weight against her. Forget whimpering, she was moaning. Begging. Her hands gripping his shirt, tugging him closer, pulling him harder as if she couldn't breathe without him.

It was when his thigh slipped between her legs that the real desperation took hold. The familiar burn making her body ache and her pulse pound. With a soft gasp, she surrendered, rolling her hips against him, chasing the friction like her life depended on it. Every slow grind sent her spiraling higher, the pressure building with each deliberate movement. Benny's guttural groan vibrated against her lips. He was urging her to take more, reminding her just how easy it was to become lost in him.

Releasing her lips, Benny's heavy breaths followed the line of her jaw, leaving a trail of fire all the way to her ear. "That's it, NeNe, take it. Take what you need." His thigh pressed into her again, harder, the pressure enough to steal air from her lungs.

Throwing her head back against the concrete, she did what she was told. More moans filled the air as Benny's mouth continued to tease her. Stubble scraped while his tongue soothed as he worked his way to the soft curve of her neck.

Jesus, Mary and Joseph.

Her skin tingled and her body burned. She was close to exploding all over Lucy's patchwork rug. So close. And when those expert lips latched on to her shoulder, she was so sure relief was just a breath away. But instead of sweet release, she could hear another voice. One that was neither hers or Benny's.

"Oh, I'm sorry, have I walked in on the past?" It was Lucy.

Crap. It's Lucy.

Her brain might have been switching back on, but she

was left aching as Benny pulled back. Strung so tight, she was genuinely worried her body would betray her, and she'd drag him back to finish the job he'd started.

Because being caught humping his leg isn't humiliating enough?

Okay. Good point.

"Uh, hey, Luce." Her hand lifted as she gave her best friend a pathetic wave.

"Lucy." Benny nodded, going on to clear his throat. "Um, I should... I should go."

Yes. He should. But she didn't want him to.

You're so fucked.

"Yeah. I reckon that's for the best," her friend replied. Giving Benny the perfect opportunity to sneak out. Not daring to utter a word or even look back at Bethany as he made a beeline for the front door.

When the heavy door slammed, the air was still crackling.

It didn't take a genius to figure out that Lucy was clearly unimpressed, her arms crossing over her chest while her head tilted in question. This was the first time Bethany had seen her friend looking remotely angry. And disappointed. Usually, her energy reflected the same warmth and ease as the golden strands of her hair.

"So?" Lucy prompted when Bethany remained silent.

"I fucked up."

"Yeah, you did. What *was* that?"

Is she talking about the humping or the kissing?

Deciding they were both equally bad, Bethany sighed. "We were fighting, about the break-up and then…"

"You fell on his face?" Wide blue eyes mocked her. "Come on, B, people don't just go from fighting to—"

"*Fucking?*" Bethany bit back a smile. "Is that the word you're looking for, Luce?"

Bethany shouldn't be finding the horror on her friend's face so funny, or the tinge of pink now splashing her cheeks. But she did. The truth was, Lucy Mills was as innocent as they came. She didn't swear, she barely drank, and she definitely wasn't having sex based off the teddy bear bed sheets in her room. She was the polar opposite of Bethany. Who was most certainly going straight to hell. Yet their friendship worked. And they'd gone from a casual friendship in school to sister-like love when Lucy had made the first of many trips out to Denver to visit her.

"You weren't…is that what you…were you going to?"

Great. She'd broken her.

Taking her friend's hand, she led them both over to the couch and gestured her down. Once comfortable, she tried her best to explain what was going on in her still very frazzled brain.

"Look, I'm not perfect." *Understatement of the year. Shut up!* "Yes, Benny and I are done. *So done.*"

"But?"

"But…it may have been a long time. *A really long time.* But it's the first time I've seen him since we broke up."

This is how you're justifying it?

Yes. It was. Because the day Benjamin Tucker broke up with her, was the last she ever saw of him. Until her wedding day. As soon as he'd told her he'd changed his mind about moving to Denver with her, she'd packed up her things and got the hell out of Woodvalley Pines and never looked back.

"And?" Even the most patient person she knew was looking more and more frustrated as creases started to furrow Lucy's porcelain brow.

"And…what I'm trying to say is that I'm not sure I ever had that *closure* that people talk about. 'Cause I never saw him again. And now…now it feels like I'm stuck in this weird-ass time warp where emotionally I've moved on but physically…physically I'm still there. Ten years ago. When I'm around him, I just can't help it, my body just does its own thing."

"*Does its own thing?*" Bethany didn't miss the skepticism in her friend's voice.

"Yes," she replied, exasperated. "It goes rogue! It's like—*why aren't we kissing? Why aren't we touching? Let me hump your leg!* I don't know." She let her eyes flutter closed. "He just brings out a side of me that I've not seen for a long time."

And that was the scary truth. Who she was when she was with Doug was very different to who she was with Benny. All this time, she'd put the difference down to growth and maturity. But what she was starting to realize was it wasn't that. Because who she was around her ex was exactly who she was when she was alone. Single. With her friends.

Just hornier.

She felt Lucy's arms wrap around her and she gladly nestled in her hold.

"Maybe don't hump his leg next time?" her friend softly teased.

"Right." She chuckled. "Baby steps."

***

"Did you hear me, Bethany?"

Bethany's eyes snapped up, her focus going back to Dr. Brunswick's flattened and wholly unimpressed lips.

"Um," she coughed. "Yes, um, *lifetime relationships*, got it." She pretended to scribble something in her notebook, hoping the older man's gray eyes had moved onto another student in the small consultation room.

It felt surreal to be back at work. And not to mention humiliating. Her morning had consisted of endless congratulations followed shortly by her awkwardly explaining to every individual person how she didn't actually end up getting married, after all.

Now here she was, at Goldacre Medical Clinic, zoning in and out during the lunchtime workshop.

"Exactly, as local physicians, we develop relationships with our patients over the course of a lifetime." Dr. Brunswick continued. "Which is why nurturing these relationships early is essential. With that in mind, I'll be assigning you each with a task designed to get you more involved with your local community."

Bethany zoned back out after that. Her mind easily wandering back to the message she'd received last night, mere hours after their kiss.

Benny: *We need to talk*

How did he even get my number?

Also, why did he still have the same number, ten years later?

They most definitely didn't need to talk. What they needed was to spend the remainder of her time in Woodvalley at least fifty yards apart at all times. Maybe even a hundred.

The only problem, of course, was that it was a small town, and her residency would keep her here another year.

You could get a place in Goldacre?

She could. Although she doubted it would make that much of a difference seeing as most Woodvalley residents frequented Goldacre to shop, eat and socialize. Woodvalley was great but it consisted of a couple of restaurants, one bar, a diner, a bakery, the Farm n' Fresh and rather randomly, a large number of antique stores.

Unable to stop herself, she sighed. A little too loud.

"Am I boring you, Bethany?"

Shit.

The next few minutes were spent attempting to convince her mentor that he had mistaken boredom for silently processing his wise words. It didn't go well.

Thankfully, by the time she'd finished humiliating herself, it was time to hand out assignments. As she stared down at the paper that had hers on it, Dr. Brunswick hovered a while longer, feeling the need to explain.

"It's a cancer survivor support group," he said. "Now and again, they have a physician stop by and answer any questions members may have, but I'd like you to go for more than one session. I want you to get to know these people. Find out their stories. Connect."

Bethany nodded. She could do that. She could sit and

listen. Connect. She was actually looking forward to it. Finally, something to take her mind off her disaster of a life.

CHAPTER SIX

Being ghosted sucked.

It's not like Benny was asking for much. After their kiss, he'd wrangled Bethany's phone number from a reluctant Mrs. Molly. He'd then proceeded to message her that they needed to talk. Because they did. When that message went unanswered, he tried again, texting her the following night.

Benny: *B, we need to talk about what happened. Meet me for a coffee this week? I'll buy.*

Nothing. Radio silence. So, he tried again the next night.

Benny: *You know, it's a small town, we're gonna bump into each other sooner or later, I'd rather things weren't awkward between us. I'm on shift for the next few days but I'll be done around 8 if you fancy grabbing a drink?*

And the next.

Benny: *I'm starting to feel like a stalker, B, can you please just reply, even if it's to tell me to fuck off?*

Even after all those messages and no reply, he was still checking his phone. Constantly. And wondering whether to text her again tonight. He'd officially reached peak pathetic.

Welcome home.

He hated how easy it had been to slip back into the pull of Bethany Mayer. She had some sort of sexy magical power over him. Even after all this time. He still wanted her. Still craved her. And he had no idea what he was supposed to do about it.

"You okay, sweetie?" His mom's hand went to his arm. "You seem rather angry with the lemon drizzle, or is it the apple tart that's done you wrong?"

A smile tugged at his lips as he lifted his gaze from the snack table to his mother. She held out a mug filled to the brim with milky coffee—just the way he liked it.

"Rough day at work?" she asked as he accepted the cup.

"I'm fine, Ma." He wasn't up for talking about Bethany. Not tonight. There would be enough emotions making an appearance as it was. Besides, this was his mother's night. "Come on, it's about to start."

Placing a hand on his mom's back, he led her over to the circle of wooden chairs. Al always made sure there was enough space for the circle, his antique collection lining the walls and corners of the store instead of taking up room in the middle.

Benny thought back to a few years ago, before Al's Antiques had begun hosting these weekly meetups, you'd have to travel two towns over to get anything like it.

As they took their seats, and waited for the meeting to start, Benny sipped on his coffee. Regretting one particular gulp as the shop door flew open. The woman doing the flinging stumbled in her heels, which meant she was hopping inside the entrance as she hollered, "Sorry, sorry. Sorry, I'm late."

Bethany frigging Mayer.

It was his only thought as coffee spray filled his vision.

What the hell is she doing here?

It was a good question. One he had an answer to sooner than he thought as Catherine, the leader of the session, quickly stood to introduce Bethany. A physician from Goldacre, here to answer any medical questions the group may have.

Fuck.

Time stood still as their gazes locked. Neither of them saying a word as they continued to stare into each other. She was shocked to see him, and she didn't hide it. He kept his eyes on her, not caring the whole room was taking in the show. They were already the talk of the town, why not pour some more gasoline on the fire.

Benny had no idea how long the inappropriate eye contact went on for, but when fake coughs became too loud to ignore, he figured it had been a while.

"What are you doing here?" Bethany finally asked, in front of everyone. "Are you...did you..."

"Have cancer?" He took pity on her as she started to get flustered. "No."

Benny felt his mom's hand on his arm at the same time as Bethany's eyes flicked to it. And then back to him.

"Y-your mom...Mrs. Tucker, shit, I mean Gloria, *you*...shit." Apparently, the fact they had an audience still hadn't sunk in. "When? How? Why didn't you—"

Benny stood, he needed to end this if not for his mom, for him. He wasn't ready to talk about this. Not with her. Not now.

"B, let's..." He gestured to the front door. "Outside?"

That's when it clicked. Frantic forest eyes went around the room as a pink flush crept up her neck. She nodded at the realization and muttered, "sorry" a few more times as she headed straight for the exit. Benny following closely behind her.

"What type?" She didn't even wait for him to reach her on the cobbles before she whipped around, looking determined.

"Breast."

"It's gone?"

"It's gone," he confirmed.

"But it came back?"

Wait. How did she—

"It came back." He swallowed hard. "A few years ago."

Bethany frowned. "When?"

"When what?"

"When was she diagnosed, when did it come back? What

was her treatment plan?"

Benny tilted his head back until he was gazing into the night sky, his patience was now relying solely on the sight of the blanket of stars above him. He got it. He knew her well enough to know this was how she processed things. She asked questions. Lots of them. She needed cold hard facts before she unleashed any sort of feelings. But knowing that didn't make this any easier.

Even as she called his name, prompting a reply, he focused on his breathing. Deep breaths in and out. When he finally turned his attention back to Bethany, her doctor mask had slipped, and the woman he remembered was staring back at him. Wide eyes glistening with concern, worry and sadness. It was enough to get him talking.

"Four years ago, it came back." He tried to keep the emotion out of his voice, but it was costing him. "Chemo, mastectomy and radiation."

Bethany nodded. "And before…when was she originally diagnosed?"

As their eyes found each other again, a charged silence hung in the air.

She knows.

Thats what her eyes told him, anyway.

"Say it." Her voice quivered.

Yep, she knows.

He still didn't want to say it. Not out loud. Which made no sense. It was a lifetime ago. Ancient history. It shouldn't matter.

But it does matter.

"Say it, Benny," she repeated. This time moisture pooled in her eyes.

His voice caught before he'd even spoken, his throat so dry he felt the need to work it.

"Before you left." There. He said it. "A few weeks before."

He should be worried by how fast his heart was beating. How hard it was to swallow. How tense his muscles suddenly felt, like they were braced for impact. But all that faded into the background as he watched Bethany draw into herself.

I'm an asshole.

A single tear trickled down her cheek and he couldn't stop himself. He went to her. Swiping the droplet with his thumb as his fingers went into her hair.

"Look at me, B," he whispered. She didn't. Couldn't. "Please, NeNe."

Her head began shaking, as she took a step back. Untangling herself from his hold.

"I have to go," she announced, still not looking at him. Slowly backing further away. "Tell Catherine I'm sorry but I had to go, I'll call her or something. I just have to…I have to—"

She didn't finish, she simply fled. Leaving him numb. This was not how she was supposed to find out.

Like you even planned on telling her.

He hated to admit it, even to himself, but that was true. There was never any plan to tell her. Not then, not now. What was the point in dragging up the past? To relive what's already happened? Inflict more pain? No. There was no point.

But now what?

It was out there. There was no taking it back.

With no immediate answers slapping him in the face, Benny sighed as he pushed open the glass door. Reluctantly, he returned to the circle, all eyes not so subtly on him as he did so. He didn't pass on Bethany's apologies to Catherine as he took his seat, nor did he address the group. He was just going to try and get through the evening as best he could while the knot in his stomach continued to twist.

His mom didn't share tonight, she listened. As did he. That didn't stop the grief from forming, though. It never failed to find him as he heard all too familiar stories from the other members of the group. Easily triggering memories he'd sooner forget.

"Benny, sweetie?" His mom's hand was back on his arm. "You, okay?"

Nope. Not one bit.

Not that he would share that. Instead, he faked composure. For his mom.

"I'm going to ask you something and you're not allowed to get upset, okay?"

He already didn't like where this was going.

"Okay," he answered slowly.

"Okay." She nodded. "I want you to speak to Bethany—"

Before she could continue, he cut her off with a, "Ma!" Not listening, she quickly waved him off.

"Let me finish, so impatient," she tsked. "I want you to go talk to that girl and bring her back here for the next session."

His mother didn't know what she was asking. There was a strong possibility Bethany Mayer might never speak to him again, let alone be in the same room as him.

"A lot of us have questions, questions only a doctor can answer, and Bethany...well, you know as well as I do, she'll be kind. Any news or advice she'll give, she'll give gently. And we need that here. A lot of us need that."

Suddenly he felt sick. "Are you? Do you think...are you feeling...?"

The words he needed were getting stuck in his throat as his mother's hand covered his.

"No, sweetie, I'm fine. I just know what it's like to be scared again and need answers. Please speak to her, son. I really think she could help a lot of people."

Benny frowned. How on earth was he going to convince Bethany to come back?

Never mind that, how the hell are you going to face her again?

Somehow, he had to make this right.

CHAPTER SEVEN

Why didn't he tell me?

Bethany was back at Lucy's and losing her mind. The same question spun through her head like some sort of answerless merry-go-round she couldn't escape.

How could something that happened so long ago make her feel like her world was about to implode? It didn't make sense. She shouldn't feel this hurt. This confused. This angry. It was freaking irrational.

"Please stop looking at Daisy-Mae like that," Lucy demanded. "*She* didn't keep a deep dark secret from you for ten years. She doesn't deserve your rage."

Bethany lifted her gaze from the ginger cat curled up by her feet so she could shoot her friend the dirty look she deserved.

Truth be told, Bethany was expecting a little more outrage from Lucy when she'd shared the news. Especially after she'd witnessed firsthand the breakup and total devastation it had caused on her first trip to Denver.

"You know, as my friend, the very least you could do is call him a dick!" Bethany whined.

"You want me to call the guy, who stayed home to look after his sick mom, with cancer, a dick?" Lucy clarified, failing to suppress a smile.

"I hate you." Bethany sulked as she slumped further

down into the couch cushions.

Another pack of Cheetos was flung at her head moments later. "Look, I get it. He should have told you. But I also understand why he didn't." Bethany's gaze lifted at her friend's more serious tone. "He was scared, B. Young and scared. And he knew you'd wanna stay with him, 'cause that's just who you are. And he didn't want that…he wanted you to live your life, follow your dreams. It's actually quite romantic."

Romantic? Clearly her friend had been binging too many romance novels again if she thought heart-shattering break-ups and ugly crying to the point of dehydration was even remotely romantic.

Suddenly, Bethany's spine snapped straight, Lucy's words sinking in. "Did you know?" she accused. "'Cause you seem to know a whole hell of a lot about why he did what he did!"

"Of course, I didn't know!" Lucy sat up too, finally showing some of the outrage Bethany expected to see earlier. "You don't have to be a genius to figure out why he did what he did, I mean, the man loved you for Pete's sake…if anything it was totally suspicious for him to just randomly change his mind about going with you, like he said he did."

"Now you tell me that!" Bethany threw the bag of chips back at Lucy's head. "Now you tell me I should have been suspicious the first-time round! You didn't think, *oh I don't know*, to tell me ten freaking years ago, when I was unable to crawl out of my dorm bed?"

Bethany was being a bitch and she knew it. She wasn't really mad at Lucy. How was her friend supposed to know what happened and why? She had her own shit to deal with when she was nineteen. But she could be mad at herself for not asking questions back then, instead, she just slinked away like a wounded stray, licking her wounds in silence.

And I can definitely be annoyed with Benny.

There was that, too.

"Why are you making that face?" Lucy asked, eyeing her warily.

Bethany rose from the cushions with enough adrenaline to make her heart hammer and her hands unsteady.

"I need answers," she declared. "And I'm going to go get them."

"It's midnight?" Lucy heckled.

Like that was going to stop her.

***

"Open up, Benny, I know you're home!"

Was this a little dramatic? Yes. Did she care? No. She'd walked out on a wedding two weeks ago—what was a little extra drama now?

Finally, the wood door flung open. "Jesus Christ, what the hell is going on? Why are you banging down my door...what time is it?"

Benny's ruffled hair stood to attention as he attempted to rub the sleep from his eyes. But it wasn't his face Bethany was looking at, not for long, anyway. Her gaze went straight to his bare chest. Correction, the six-pack that had replaced it.

Where the hell did that come from?

"My eyes are up here, B."

She didn't miss the amusement in his voice, yet it wasn't quite enough to muster the willpower to drag her eyes away.

Benny had always had a good body, sure, and yes, she wasn't blind, she'd noticed he'd bulked up. But thinking it and seeing it were two very different things.

Wow.

"B?"

"Shush." Yes. She shushed him. She was concentrating.

"Are you being serious, right now?" Benny tried again.

Is that one of those V muscles?

"B?"

This wasn't fair. The dumpee is the one who gets a

revenge body, not the person administering the dumping. When she was done looking her fill, she was angry again. Irrationally angry.

"You suck!" Benny wisely didn't reply beyond a lip twitch as she went on to tell him why exactly he sucked. "You actually have the audacity to show up to my wedding looking all fucking—" she gestured her hand down the length of him. "*All fucking hot.* Giving me a lift when I needed one. Being nice to me when I was a bitch. And tonight—tonight you took away the *one* thing that was keeping me sane. My right to be mad. *Mad* you left me. *Mad* you broke my heart. I don't get to be angry at you anymore and it's not fair. 'Cause what am I supposed to do with all that hurt? Where am I supposed to put it? *Where*, Benny, *where?*"

Her hands were up in the air now flailing, officially solidifying her crazy lady look. "And that damn kiss, what the fuck was that? Where do you get off kissing me like that? Making me want you again? How dare you! You ought to——"

At some point, Benny had moved closer, close enough that his lips slamming down onto hers only registered as her moan echoed in the darkness.

Fuck me.

He was doing it again. Kissing her like she was his. Setting her body alight and making her poor, battered heart skip too many beats than it could handle.

Wrapping her arms around his neck, she tugged him closer, clinging on for dear life, swallowing his groans like they were the only thing keeping her alive.

As his hands went to her hips, she started to ache from the want. And when his fingers dipped further, digging into flesh as he hauled her up, not even the pounding in her ears could drown out the desperate need spiraling through her as she wrapped her legs around his torso.

Between teasing swipes of his tongue and the intense press of his body, it was hard to pinpoint when exactly he'd taken her inside. The cold surface of the wall did register, though as her flimsy sundress was hiked over her head and discarded while she gasped for air.

She welcomed the chill, helping unclasp her bra as the heat of her skin became unbearable.

Losing his mouth, it wasn't long before she felt it again. The bristle of his stubble scorching her neck as she felt her panties being pushed to the side. When his lips locked onto the curve, her head flung back, a ragged whimper filling the air as he sucked just enough to mark her. The pleasure and pain blurring her senses and making her more desperate.

"Take me," she panted. "I need you. Take me."

Sparks shot through her veins as he positioned himself between her thighs, but he didn't move, not to where she wanted him. He teased. His hips rocking. His teeth dragging. And the slickness of his heated skin rubbing.

"You're dripping for me, aren't you, NeNe?" He didn't wait for her answer before dipping his head and latching onto her hardened nipple. *Fuck.* She felt herself shudder as he sucked, his teeth teasing and tugging as she writhed against him. It was the rough drag of his fingers entering her that had a cry escaping her, though as her head tipped back.

"So fucking wet and needy. Such a good fucking girl for me." His voice was getting grittier. Raspier.

Coming out of her skin with need, she moaned. A moan that managed to summon Benny's lips as they covered her mouth once again. While his kiss gave her slow and soft, his controlled strokes inside her quickly turned punishing.

Her body pulsated. Her core drenched. She was going to lose her mind if he didn't take her in the next thirty seconds. It was that frantic need that had her pulling back, making her demand through choppy breaths.

"Please, Benny. I need you. Take me. Take it like it's yours."

She knew those words would do it. She was rewarded with a low growl rumbling from his chest seconds later as his mouth claimed hers again and his fingers were replaced with what she really wanted. And with one brutal thrust, he reminded her just how good it felt to be his. And, just how dangerous.

***

There were not enough curse words in the universe for Bethany to communicate just how utterly dumb she was.

And embarrassed, don't forget embarrassed.

How could she? Not while she was lying on her best friend's couch, still homeless, fresh out of an engagement and covered in her ex-boyfriend's scent.

Is this rock bottom?

It felt like it. Especially when she was in such a rush to run out on Benny, after they'd done the deed, that she hadn't even bothered to put on her bra. She was getting far too good at running. She'd been in her car less than a minute after he'd been inside her.

Classy.

Throwing the blanket over her head, she let out a groan. When had it gotten this bad? Only a month ago she was planning a wedding, her life, excited about what the future held. Her head was filled with paint swatches, kitchen cabinet designs, and potential baby rooms. Now? Now all she could think about was Benny. How things could have been so different if he'd only told her about his mom. How good that kiss was. How damn right he felt inside her. And worst of all, all she could think about doing was driving back over to his house for round two.

I'm totally screwed.

She was. And to top it all off, tomorrow, she had to explain to her supervisor why she'd run out of a cancer survivors support group and not returned.

Great.

CHAPTER EIGHT

Take it like it's yours.

To say Benny was distracted was the understatement of the century. Less than twenty-four hours ago he'd taken his ex-girlfriend up against a wall and now, here he was, in his friend's backyard, pretending his head wasn't fucked while everyone around him celebrated.

"Crazy shit, right?" Zach saddled up beside him, beer in hand as he nodded over at the happy couple.

The happy couple were Cat and Cody, who had just announced they were pregnant. They already had a ten-year-old son together, and despite not being his biological mom, Cat, had quickly claimed Dylan as her own.

All the gang were here today. His friend Hunter and his wife Rachel. Luke and his girlfriend Bella. Wade, who was one of Zach's brothers, and his girlfriend Riley. Then there were Zach's other brothers, Matt and Jonah who helped Wade run the Evans ranch.

The baby news wasn't a shock, not really. Cat loved being a mom and never hid the fact she wanted a house full of children. Benny was happy for them. Despite what his face probably looked like.

"You good?" Zach asked when he didn't reply.

He wasn't good. He was going out of his mind. Which is likely why he opened his big mouth.

"I slept with Bethany," he blurted.

"Today?"

"What? No! Last night. It happened last night."

"And that's better?" Zach joked. Benny glared. Unimpressed at the huge grin on his friend's face. "Man, for someone who just got laid—"

"Don't say it," he warned.

Zach held up his hands in surrender. "Okay, okay. All I'm trying to say is I'm surprised. That's all. I thought you'd be much happier when the time finally came."

When the time finally came? What was he talking about? Which is exactly what he asked him next.

Zach offered a nonchalant shrug. "We all knew it was only a matter of time."

They all knew? "Don't tell me you assholes had bets on this shit? 'Cause that's messed up!"

"Hey, chill." Zach put away his dimples and turned more serious. "Of course, we didn't have bets on this. We just know you, man. We were there when you got that wedding invite. We were there when you beat the shit out of the punch bag at the gym after. And we were there biting our tongues when we found out she ended up back at your place the night of her wedding. We're not stupid, we know how you feel about the girl."

"You bit your tongues?" Benny raised a brow.

"Fine, *some of us* bit our tongues more than others." Zach's smile was back as he pushed floppy blond hair from his face.

It was hard to stay mad at Zach. Not when he knew just how much he cared about his friends and had no problem showing it. Luke was much easier to be pissed at. The sarcastic bastard. And Hunter, too. The big man may not talk much but when he did, he knew exactly what to say to hit a nerve.

Blowing out a long breath, Benny tried to remember what the point was of this sharing session.

Brain leakage?

Sounded about right. That and he was confused. Frustrated. And horny as hell. Which meant he needed advice. And out of all of his friends, Zach was the easiest to ask.

"I don't know what she wants," Benny admitted.

Zach nodded before asking, "Do you know what *you* want?"

Not having a frigging clue, Benny shook his head.

"So...the idea of you guys getting back together hasn't crossed your mind?"

Benny's jaw tightened at the question. Taking another swig of his beer, he attempted to control his heartrate.

It was only natural to think about 'what if' when an ex comes back into your life, right?

Because you're such an expert?

He was starting to see the issue of nearing thirty-years old with only one real relationship under his belt. The truth was, he had no idea what he was supposed to be feeling. Was it normal to still consider Bethany his after all this time? Because he did. Last night only solidified that feeling. To him, taking her felt right. She belonged to him. And he wanted to do it again. And again. And again.

Yeah, try explaining that to Zach without sounding like a deluded, possessive, sex-crazed asshole.

Instead, he went for a more watered-down version. "I don't know if this is gonna make sense, but it feels like she never stopped being mine."

Thankfully, Zach didn't look shocked. If anything, he looked thoughtful as he nodded to himself.

"I get it." *Thank God someone does.* "I felt that way with Libby...like she was mine, even when she wasn't." Great, he wasn't some kind of freak. Hallelujah. "You want my advice?" The desperation must have been shining in Benny's eyes because Zach continued without him having to say anything. "Don't fight it. Don't run. Do what feels right for you and I promise...things will fall into place."

"You sound like a fucking fortune cookie, dude. Speak

English."

The dimples were back out. "Okay, let's just say, if you just so happen to end up with Bethany in your bed again, just go with it. Don't get caught up in the details of what's going to happen next. Lean into it. See where it goes."

Okay. This was advice he could get behind. No overthinking. Bethany in his bed again. He didn't know what he liked more.

Who the fuck are you kidding?

Fine. Maybe it wasn't so hard to choose. Not after what they did and how damn good it felt. So good that he was worried she'd already well and truly ruined him for any other woman. Despite that extremely alarming side effect, the idea of doing what they did last night again was enough to get his blood heating and his mood brightening.

Lean into it…see where it goes.

How hard could it be?

"Theres something else," Benny announced, his stomach already somersaulting. "Last night, well, last night, she found out the real reason I broke up with her."

He'd never told anyone. His friends knew about his mom's cancer. Although they'd learned about the first time she was diagnosed much later as he'd joined the fire department only a few months into her treatment and hadn't exactly felt like sharing with his new colleagues.

"Shit, man. I just assumed she broke up with you." Zach was trying his best to hide his smile. It wasn't working. Fucker.

His friend was treated to a whack on the arm. "Thanks, asshole."

"Hey, you're the one acting all lovesick. I just assumed. We all did. So…you gonna put me out of my misery? Why did you break up with her?"

"Between us?" Zach lifted his chin in acknowledgement, his stare back to serious in the blink of an eye. "My mom's first diagnosis was a few weeks before I was set to follow her to Denver. And I just couldn't do it. I couldn't leave my mom."

"And you never told her why?" Zach looked suitably horrified, only making him feel guiltier when he shook his head in reply. "Jesus, man."

It was a minute before his friend spoke again, and when he did, he knew what was coming.

"That is the one thing you will have to talk about, you know that, right? She deserves to have that talk."

He was right. She did deserve it. He just had no idea how he could possibly justify not telling her.

"I know. Shit. I know."

***

Benny's hand on the laminate door stilled. Taking a moment, he drew in a deep breath.

What's the plan, again?

He'd woken up determined. Fire in his belly. With a mission to complete. But now, now he was questioning himself. Having second thoughts.

I'm gonna fuck this up.

It had been two days since Cat and Cody's celebration, and Zach's advice was still fresh in his mind. Combine his friend's words with the fact Benny was still unable to think of anything else, and the desperation to see Bethany again was almost unbearable. Which was how he found himself at the Goldacre Medical Clinic, making an appointment under Hunter's name.

You can do this. Stick to the plan.

There wasn't really a plan per se. He'd decided this morning to focus specifically on Zach's idea to go with the flow. Not that making an appointment to see Bethany under his friend's name was very 'go with the flow', it wasn't, but it was either this or get ghosted again. And being ghosted really freaking sucked.

So, there he was, pushing open the door and taking an apprehensive step into the sleek and incredibly shiny consultation room.

Bethany's eyes went comically wide at the sight of him. "What are you—"

Knowing exactly what she was going to say, he quickly interjected. "We need to talk."

At his announcement, he didn't miss her slowly backing up against the gray wall behind her. It was her outfit, though, that had him doing a double take. Sexy white lab coat. Figure hugging black dress that went all the way down to her knees. Not so sensible black heels. And a damn stethoscope draped around her neck, taunting him. Because yes, he was weak, and his schoolboy brain was already conjuring up X-rated fantasies of them playing doctor.

Yes, please.

"Please tell me Hunter Campbell is sitting out there, waiting for his appointment, and you didn't just commit insurance fraud so you could come in here and tell me *we need to talk?*"

Well, when she put it like that? Shit.

"Oh my God!" She stomped when he didn't answer quick enough. "What the fucking, fuck, Benny?"

She was no longer backing up. She was rounding her desk, untangling her stethoscope and flinging it over her shoulder as she marched toward him.

"Is that the language you use with all your patients, doctor?" He couldn't help himself. Clearly.

A cute growl escaped her lips as she slammed the door shut behind him, quickly spinning back around to face him.

"You're unbelievable, Benny."

"Unbelievable?" he repeated, a smug smirk forming. He shouldn't be enjoying this. Shouldn't be so turned on. But he was. "Funny, I seem to recall you saying the same thing to me the other night. When I had your legs shaking so hard you were scared you couldn't stand up." Like a douche, he added a wink.

You're going to hell.

"You've got to be kidding me!" Narrowed eyes cut to

him.

He took a step forward. Admiring Bethany's sexy scowl. Not missing the heat darkening her gaze. She looked torn between kissing him and killing him. So, he made the choice for her, closing the distance between them before she could decide.

Benny's hand went to her waist as he hauled her close, his mouth slamming down onto hers as he worked to pry sugary pink lips apart. It didn't take long. On a gasp, she melted into his touch, teasing his tongue with tentative swipes of her own. She tasted like caramel coffee. Fucking delicious.

Backing her up to the nearest wall, it was only when she was trembling that he suddenly remembered the other thing he came here to do, and momentarily broke their kiss. His mouth still brushing hers as he made his demand through heavy breaths.

"You're going back to the support group. This week."

"Okay. Yes," she readily agreed. Impatiently taking his mouth again, her hands wrapping around his neck as she tugged him closer.

That was easier than he thought. She really did want this as much as he did. That thought alone made his blood heat further, driving him deeper into her.

The feel of her supple body pressing into him had his hands moving. One skimming over the swell of her chest, pausing just long enough to feel her nipple tighten beneath his touch. The other trailed over silky curves, dipping lower until he found her ass, where he took a firm and greedy handful.

Goddamn beautiful.

He needed more. He needed her dress off and her legs spread. He wanted to taste her creamy skin as his fingers worked her. Until she was slick. Ready. And desperate.

With a new mission in mind, he shifted his hands, this time he was searching for a zipper. A way in. But he came up short.

Damnit.

Releasing her plump lips, he spoke into her again. "You've got three seconds to get your perfect ass out of this dress, or I'm ripping it."

He was gifted with a sultry, lopsided smile, her eyes glossy as her lab coat slid to the floor. Easing back, she reached behind, her fingers quick to find the cleverly hidden zipper. More fabric pooled at her feet as he took the sight of her in and worked his newly tightened throat.

Black lace barely contained her curves, sky high-heels making her legs look even longer. But it was her face that did it. Broke any control he had left. Swollen, wet lips pushing out broken breaths as dark green eyes heated.

"Your turn," she challenged.

His shirt was over his head a second later, smug satisfaction warming his chest as more fire sparked in her eyes. Once he'd kicked off his boots, his jeans were next to go, then his boxers.

As tempting as it was to take her right then and there, he wasn't going to. Not yet. He'd already had her against a wall. Rough, how they both liked it. But today? Today he wanted something else. He wanted to take his time. They had some catching up to do that involved dragging his mouth over every inch of her. He wanted her to shake. Plead. Writhe. Only then would he take what was his.

Dropping to his knees, he threw one leg over his shoulder, his mouth going straight to her center. Moments later, his tongue was eagerly taking its first swipe of sweetness. Ignoring Bethany's muffled gasp, a smile tugged at his lips as he felt her back hit the wall and her body arch. It was when her hands laced through his hair, though, that he lost it.

His grip on her thighs tightened, his leisurely strokes quickly becoming hungrier. Ten long years he'd been starved. He was going to take every drop she gave him. And that's what he did. His mouth relentless as he felt her body ripple and buck. She was chasing every flick of his tongue, cursing his name while begging for more. This was the Bethany he remembered. Wild. Free. Mine.

CHAPTER NINE

"Shit," Bethany muttered on a stumble. She was trying to shimmy back into her dress, her legs apparently still shaking enough to affect her balance.

Multiple orgasms will do that to a girl.

It was official, she was out of control. Sex with an ex once wasn't great. But twice? Twice was catastrophically stupid. Even for her.

Don't forget at work. You did it at work, too. Anyone could have walked in.

Frigging marvelous. Another curse left her lips as she finally managed to close the zipper. She was a dumbass.

"B, baby." Benny's hand cupped her cheek as she desperately tried to look anywhere else but into his eyes. "Don't be mad. Please."

Her gaze went down and she immediately regretted it. The damn man was still shirtless. Flashing that hard chest at her again. He was temptation wrapped up in a six-pack sent personally to wreck her.

"NeNe, look at me." She was. That was part of the problem. On a sigh, she met his eyes. "We're going to do that again," he confidently declared.

What did he just say?

She was mentally preparing to open a full can of whoop ass on him when he went on, his thumb lazily stroking her cheek. "Don't give me that look and pretend you weren't chanting my name five minutes ago." *The freaking nerve.* "'Cause you were. Just like I was chanting yours when you clamped down around me and I saw fucking stars."

She was finding it hard to swallow as she stared into him, the intensity in his eyes scaring the living daylights out of her.

"Tell me this won't happen again," he demanded.

Opening her mouth to try, she thought better of it and changed her mind. She'd already proved she had absolutely zero willpower, best not make herself a liar, too.

"That's what I thought." A dangerous smile tilted his lips before his mouth covered hers again.

Yep. Zero willpower. At least you're consistent.

Another claiming kiss sent more shivers through her. She also might've accidentally moaned again as he opened her up to him. Killing more brain cells as he tasted every inch of her.

Just as she was contemplating repeating her stupidity for a third time, a loud knock on the consultation door had her heart stopping for an entirely different reason.

Damnit. At work, remember?

How could she keep forgetting?

Quickly slipping from Benny's hold, she crouched down to pick up her white jacket.

"Can I come in?" Dr. Brunswick's deep voice echoed through the wood.

"Um," she stuttered, trying her best to redress and flatten her sex hair. "I'm in the middle of a physical exam."

Benny flashed her a wicked grin at her announcement, clearly in no hurry to put a shirt on.

"Male or Female?" Brunswick asked.

"Male," she confirmed hesitantly.

"Great."

Next thing she knew, Dr. Brunswick was pushing open the door.

Is this what a stroke feels like?

She couldn't feel her legs. A cold sweat breaking out as her supervisor approached. Ignoring the topless man, his gaze flicked between Bethany and the clipboard he was holding.

"Sorry to interrupt, but how much longer do you think you'll need? We're getting a bit backed up out there and I need to know whether to reassign some of your patients."

She was guessing that she'd gone way over the allotted fifteen minutes with Benny.

"I'm sorry," she rushed out. Clearly flustered. "I'm almost done. Just need to wrap up here."

Dr. Brunswick sent a reassuring smile Benny's way and gave her a nod. "Take your time. I've got the next patient covered, just let me know when you're finished."

It was only after Brunswick left the room that she could breathe again. Oh no. Could he tell what she'd been doing? Had she been loud? Did everyone in reception hear her chanting her ex-boyfriend's name?

Oh my God. Oh my God.

She was still spiraling when Benny's hands came to her face again. "Hey. B. It's okay. He had no idea. Trust me."

Sure. Trust her ex who had broken her heart. Lied about why he'd dumped her. And tricked her into sex. Twice.

Tricked?

Okay. Maybe not tricked. Still, he did keep flashing those abs at her. That was just as bad. Speaking of which—she released herself to pick up his shirt and throw it at him.

"*You!* You need to go. Right now. And don't even think about turning up here again."

She was gifted with another smoldering smile as he shrugged the material over his head. "Dinner at my place, Friday?"

Had he taken a knock to the head?

"Out!" she hissed, her finger going to the door.

"Okay, baby." He lay a quick kiss on her lips before backing up toward the exit. "I'll call you."

Finally alone, she swiped the phone from her desk. She

was in over her head, clearly. It was time to call in reinforcements.

***

Bethany had managed to convince Lucy to take a trip to the Tipsy Cow with her after work. It was Woodvalley's one and only bar. A neon-lit cave where the walls were plastered with a rather random assortment of glowing signs. And while it was a perfectly acceptable establishment, her friend had felt the need to remind her several times that she wasn't a 'bar person' because it reminded her too much of work. Apparently, serving food at the diner was dangerously close to sitting at a bar with her friend.

After promising she'd never drag Lucy back there, Bethany confessed her sins. Coming clean about not just one but two trysts with Benny. Luckily, she had a big glass of red wine to help her through the conversation.

As expected, Lucy was horrified.

"Please close your mouth, Luce. People are looking."

Well, not really. A couple of older cowboys perched at the bar may have given them a quick glance when they'd arrived, but nothing since then. Still, she really needed Lucy to stop gaping at her.

"I just...in the consultation room?"

That was the part she was stuck on? "Yes. And the other night when I went over to his place."

She should have told Lucy after that night, but she'd been too embarrassed. Now, here she was, shoveling more shame onto the shitshow that was her life.

"Lucy!" a woman's voice called out. "I never see you here!" Was she British?

Thirty seconds later and Bethany had her answer as an attractive, dark-haired woman with a gentle curve to her belly stood at their high-top table wrapping Lucy up into a warm embrace.

"I can't believe it; I've been trying to drag your arse here for months. I see I'm just gonna have to be more convincing next time." The woman straightened, her gaze going straight to Bethany as she outstretched a hand. "Hi. I'm Cat, and you're Bethany, right...the runaway bride?"

The runaway bride? Jesus Christ.

Lucy laughed. *Traitor.*

"Congratulations by the way," her friend was quick to add, before Bethany had a chance to confirm whether she was or wasn't the runaway bride. "Rachel told me the news. I'm so happy for you, Cody and Dylan." Her friend's eyes went to the bump.

Bethany watched Cat visibly soften as she placed a protective hand over her belly. "Thanks, Lucy. We're all really excited."

"There you are!" another female voice hollered, this one she recognized.

Rachel. The petite redhead who'd helped secure her bags.

"Bethany!" Rachel beamed as she joined them at the table. "It's so good to see you, sugar."

Bethany could see the woman meant it and that was enough for her to relax a little.

A few minutes later, Cat and Rachel had pulled up stools to join them. They obviously already knew Lucy from Molly's Diner where she worked, but they'd also begun filling her in on how they knew each other, too.

So far, she'd learned Cat was married to Cody, who was best friends with Zach Evans, who worked with Benny. She remembered Zach, he was the oldest of the four Evans brothers, the youngest of which: Jonah, she'd gone to school with. Bethany already knew Rachel was married to Hunter who also worked with Benny, but they also mentioned another guy, Luke, who worked with them too, and was part of the same enormous friendship group. As was Luke's girlfriend Bella, Zach's wife Libby, Wade: another Evans brother and his girlfriend Riley.

I should probably be writing this down.

Being away so long, it had been easy to forget just how interconnected her small town was. Everyone knew each other, literally, and each other's business.

"So, how come you ran out on your wedding?" Cat asked, a little too casually.

Bethany had been about to take a sip of her wine when she paused mid tip.

Straight to it, then.

Usually, she wouldn't take kindly to strangers so openly prying. But there was something about the extremely blunt Cat that stopped her from being offended. Granted, she'd only known her five minutes, but like Rachel, there was something so real and genuine about the woman. It was almost as if she was asking out of concern rather than curiosity. It was for that reason, Bethany opened up.

"Well," she cleared her throat, placing the wine glass back on the scratched wood table. "I was standing there in my wedding dress, looking in the mirror. *Really* looking. And asked myself one question. One question that I knew would be the difference between me saying I do or getting the hell out of there."

All the women leaned in, their elbows hitting the wood as their eyes widened in anticipation.

"What was the question?" Cat prodded.

She gave the women surrounding her a sad smile. "I asked myself, if there was no one out there, no packed church, no expectant parents…would I still go through with it?"

Rachel gasped in wonder. Cat nodded in understanding. While Lucy matched her own sad smile.

On that note, it was time for another round. One hour passed and as a second glass of wine made it into her system, Bethany participated in another sharing session.

She spoke about Denver and her residency, and in turn, Rachel told her more about her bakery, Fairy Baked. Cat talked about working as a book editor, while Lucy, as usual, stayed quiet, only perking up once at the mention of the new romance book Cat was reading.

Note to self, remind Lucy how awesome she is and encourage her to share that awesomeness with others.

"What's it like seeing Benny again?" Rachel innocently batted her eyelashes. "You two dated in high school, didn't you?"

Bethany's eyes shot to Lucy who was nervously biting her lip. Then her gaze landed on Cat who all of a sudden was finding her chipped red nail varnish fascinating.

Oh my God. They know.

She didn't know how they knew, but she felt it immediately. Talk about a giant elephant in the room.

"Okay, come on. Spill it." Bethany banged both hands down onto the table. "What do you know?" Her eyes flicked between Rachel and Cat as they both sported guilty expressions.

"She's good," Cat was quick to point out.

"I know you know something, so let's just get it all out there," Bethany continued.

Rachel wasn't meeting her eyes. Cat went back to looking at her nails. Surprisingly, Lucy was the one to pipe up.

"Come on, ladies. B needs to know what the Woodvalley gossip mill is saying about her. If it was the other way around, you'd want to know, too."

Bethany mouthed a thank you to her friend and reached over to squeeze her hand. See, Lucy was awesome.

Cat sighed. "The Woodvalley gossip mill knows nothing, I swear." *Yeah, right.* "Only me, Rachel and Libby know. No one else, I promise. Not even Bella or Riley and let me tell you, they'll be royally pissed off when they find out we knew and didn't tell them."

She wasn't thrilled to hear that Cat thought the other women were going to find out, but the other stuff she said didn't sound too awful. "Are you going to tell me what you, Rachel and Libby know, or do I need to find you a pen so you can draw me a picture?"

Cat's laughter sliced through some of the tension now thickening the air.

"I knew I liked you," she smirked. "Okay. Fine. Don't be mad. But Benny told Zach about you guys...you know...doing the deed." *Fucking Benny.* "And Zach tells his wife everything. She, of course, told me because we also tell each other everything...and Rachel *might* have overheard us."

On cue, Rachel flashed her another guilty look.

Okay. This wasn't a disaster. The town didn't know. Just a few people in Benny's friendship group. It could be worse.

"Wait." Bethany waved a finger at the women across from her. "Do all the guys know, too? I take it you tell your husbands everything, too?"

Oh, for fucks sake.

She clearly didn't need verbal confirmation. Their faces said it all.

"We suck. I get it," Cat declared. "But we love Benny. And we've never seen him react to any woman the way he reacts to you." Rachel was nodding right along with her friend's words. "We just don't want to see him get hurt, that's all."

Benny get hurt? Oh, please.

Bethany let out a noise that conveyed just how ridiculous she thought that statement was. It was a cross between a snort and pfft.

"You know that he was the one to break up with *me*, right? He broke *my* heart. If anything, I'm the one who stands to get broken all over again here...not him."

Rachel's hand went to Bethany's arm. "We didn't know, sugar. No one told us anything. The first we heard of your existence was a few months ago when Benny got your wedding invite." She still couldn't believe her parents had sent an invite to her ex-boyfriend. Talk about inappropriate. "So, tell us. How long were you together, why'd you break up...start at the beginning."

The beginning? Damnit. She was going to need another

drink.

CHAPTER TEN

"Ow!" Benny complained, a hand shooting to the side of his head where Rachel had just flung a giant bag of mixed nuts at him.

"Oops," she cooed, before disappearing back into the kitchen to join the others.

That was the third thing she'd chucked at his head since he'd arrived at Cat and Cody's twenty minutes ago. He was starting to think she was doing it on purpose.

"Is there a reason your wife is attacking me with family-sized snack-bags today?" He turned to Hunter who looked incredibly relaxed, his hulking frame reclining in the leather armchair opposite him.

He'd signed up for pizza and a movie, not to be an angry females target practice.

"Think carefully...do you *really* want to know? Or do you want to have a nice, quiet, drama-free night?"

What the fuck?

"Yes, dude. I *really* want to know why your wife is trying really damn hard to give me a concussion."

Hunter grimaced, looking personally offended by the prospect of having an actual conversation. Not that Benny could blame him, they'd been on shift together all week, and to say it had been busy would be putting it mildly. Spring had officially sprung with record breaking temperatures, and with the heat brought an onslaught of brush fires. It was brutal. They all deserved a night in. To kick back, watch a movie and drink a beer or two. And not have to worry about weaponized junk food.

He watched as his friend scrubbed a big hand down his face. "Rachel ran into Bethany at the Tipsy Cow the other night."

"And?" Benny huffed. Impatience already starting to gnaw.

He ignored the tick in his jaw at the mention of Bethany. Resisted the urge to pull out his phone and check to see if she'd replied to his latest unanswered message. And refused to acknowledge the way his fingers itched to text her again.

Do it and she's gonna get a restraining order on your ass.

Letting out a sigh, his patience continued to be tested as Cat and Cody entered the room hand in hand. Benny's eyes went to them as they lowered themselves onto the overstuffed brown leather couch, Cat's fingers quickly going to a belly that had practically appeared overnight.

"Pizza should be here in thirty," Cody announced, his gaze flicking between the two men. "You guys good?"

Trust Cody to realize immediately that he walked into something. It was probably a cop thing.

Neither of the men spoke, unless you count Hunter grunting. Benny simply rolled his eyes and averted his gaze. Their conversation would just have to wait. Cody didn't bother calling them out, his attention was back to Cat, his own hand joining hers on the bump as he gave her a serene smile.

I'm gonna hurl.

Sure, he was happy for his friends. But for the first time ever, he felt like the odd one out. The single one. Maybe it was all the confusing shit that was happening with Bethany. Or maybe it was the fact that everyone was moving on with their lives and he was just standing still. All he knew was things that never bothered him before were starting to sting. Like the constant public displays of affection.

You probably should have thought of that before you agreed to spend the evening with three couples.

Yeah. He should have.

Talking of which, Rachel joined them next. Going straight to Hunter's lap and curling herself into him. Libby and Zach followed, taking a seat on the couch beside him.

"So, what are we watching?" Benny asked as all the couples seemed to snuggle into one another.

"Why, you worried you can't commit the time to it already?" Cat snarked.

What the fuck?

"Excuse me?" Benny's head snapped in her direction.

Narrowed blue eyes closed in on him. "I was simply asking...given your history, if you were concerned that you may not be able to commit to a whole two-hour movie."

"What the hell is that supposed to mean?"

"Careful," Cody warned. Not enjoying the irritation in Benny's tone.

"It means, you're a coward Benjamin Tucker. I know all about the hit and run you pulled on Bethany."

He was quickly putting two and two together. Rachel *and* Cat ran into Bethany at the Tipsy Cow and apparently had a good old chat about their breakup.

"Jesus Christ, not you as well! Aren't y'all supposed to be *my* friends? Where's the goddamn loyalty?"

Cat's finger came up. "Don't mess with me, Tucker, I'm pregnant, therefore I can legally murder you."

"I'm not sure that's how it works, kitten," Cody interjected, clearly amused and not at all concerned by his wife's homicidal threat.

Zach also finally found his voice and lifted the palm of his hand that had been resting on Libby's shoulder. "Come on guys, enough. Benny's right. He's *our* friend first. So let's maybe stop launching things at his head." Zach's gaze darted to Rachel who quickly looked away. "Threatening murder." Blue eyes went to Cat next who simply glared back. "And hear his side of the story?"

Great. Just what I wanted. I get to share.

All eyes went to him expectantly. He hadn't had enough beer for this. He was also still struggling to justify what he did all those years ago. It didn't have to end the way it did. He was just scared. He didn't know how to handle what was happening. And he didn't want to drag Bethany down the black hole he'd already jumped down. He thought he was doing the right thing. Thought it was all for the best. How was he supposed to know how much hurt he'd cause. How much regret he'd feel. And how a decade later, she'd still own his heart.

With no excuses in sight, he laid it all out for his friends and hoped for the best.

***

"Clear!" Luke yelled. The crack of breaking glass cutting through the thick air.

Sticky heat clung to Benny's forehead as he dropped to his knees. Sweat trickling freely now. Thank God, Zach, their team EMT was next to him. Shielding the woman they were trying desperately to free of broken glass while reassuring her everything was going to be okay. By the looks of the fuel leaking under the car, time wasn't on their side, and he needed to concentrate.

Carefully, he wedged the metal tips of the spreaders between the car door and mangled frame. One switch, one turn, and the hissing started as the hydraulic tool began biting metal. His eyes focused on the warped door, the slow inching outward of it until finally with a jolt, it gave way.

"Let's get you outta here, darlin'."

She was in his arms in one swoop, his pace quickly turning to a jog toward the waiting ambulance. His team members were jogging too, at his side, calling for everyone to get back. And that's when he felt it, heat scorching the sky. One more second in that car and they'd all be fucked.

Letting his team handle the burning car behind him, he

continued on. No paramedics were in sight as he reached the vehicle. Placing the older woman on the ledge, he searched the surroundings, his gaze immediately landing on the one person he wasn't expecting to find. Bethany. *What the hell?* Jade eyes held him hostage as she stared at him. Both their breathing picking up pace as he took his first step toward her.

"B?" he rasped. "What are you doing here?" It was her turn to take a step, and when she did, he got a glimpse of tear-stained cheeks. Whipping his helmet off, he closed the distance between them, his fingers slipping into the loose waves at the nape of her neck, his thumb sweeping along her jaw. "Baby, what's wrong? Are you hurt? Did one of the cars—"

Her head vehemently shook. "No, I-I was on my way to work and…"

Christ almighty.

They'd been called to the pile up an hour ago. One drunk driver on the highway between Woodvalley and Goldacre had caused a whole load of shit. Ten cars in total were affected. It was a miracle no one had been seriously injured.

"You wanna take a look, Doc?"

Benny recognized that voice, it was Carla, one of the Goldacre paramedics. He turned to find the petite blond already checking the patient's vitals. Her ponytail whipped as she went from checking her heartrate to wrapping the blood pressure cuff around her arm.

"Uh, yeah," Bethany replied, quickly untangling herself and rounding Benny.

"You're working?" he blurted.

The face she gave him said it all. "I'm a doctor who was first on the scene. Of course, I'm working. Paramedics are stretched and you've got *one* EMT."

He could only watch as she turned her back on him. Unable to move. Whatever he'd seen in her eyes just moments ago was gone. Her focus was only on the woman in front of her. Like a lovestruck idiot, he couldn't look away. If anything, he was staring. Which meant he didn't miss the care and the kindness that went into every touch, every check and every word she uttered.

Goddamn she's perfect.

His hand went to his chest—where he checked for wounds. Cuts. A huge fucking knife, because the ache in his heart wasn't easing. And he was no closer to feeling his legs.

He didn't catch what Bethany said to Carla. Or the words she shouted over to Steve, the other paramedic treating a head wound on the curb. He was too busy gazing into deep green when she turned back around. Eyes still misty as she marched back over to him.

A soft palm landed on his chest seconds later. He was still standing in the same place she'd left him. His helmet tucked under his arm. His heart beating way too damn fast as all the *what ifs* circled in his head.

"I saw you," she whispered, as if she was sharing a secret.

"What?" he rasped.

"I saw you. I saw you break open the car. I saw you get that woman out. And then I saw...I saw the car set on fire." She audibly gulped. Wide eyes boring into him as her hand skimmed his chest. Next thing he knew, dainty fingers were wrapping around his neck and tugging him close. The taste of burnt roses filling his lungs as soft, warm lips brushed against his. "Kiss me, Benny."

Letting his helmet drop to the ground, his hands lifted, cupping her cheeks. He made sure her eyes were on him. "No more fucking games." His voice felt raw as the words scraped his throat. "I mean it, NeNe. If we're doing this, *you're mine.*"

Green fire sparked, but he resisted the urge to surrender to the flames. Not until, "I'm yours" slipped from her perfect pink lips.

And damnit, it was worth the wait.

CHAPTER ELEVEN

Bethany faintly heard the sounds of whoops and cheers while she continued to get lost in the man in front of her. She clung to him. Reveling in every swipe of his tongue, every angle he moved her, and every goosebump he administered.

Yes, it was crazy. Yes, she should definitely get her head checked. She'd gone out of her way to avoid Benny all week. Depriving herself of the addictive coffee from Molly's Diner and resisting a trip to Fairy Baked to sample some of their delicious cakes. She'd even called his mother to check to see if he'd be attending the support group this week, only confident enough to turn up when she'd found out he was on shift. Then, of course, there were all the messages she'd ignored.

Watching a hot firefighter risk his life and save the day would be enough for most, but it was the thought of losing him all over again that made her insides twist. Had her heart leaping out of her chest. And her hands ready to wrap around him and hold on tight.

So, she has no idea what she's doing. Who cares there's no plan? After witnessing how quickly everything could change, she'd decided that all that matters is the here. The now. The earthy musk filling her throat. The press of Benny's hand on the small of her back, plastering her body to his. And the possessive growl she was currently swallowing, making her chest pound and her panties wet.

"Dude!" a deep voice called, closer this time. "Are you freaking serious, right now? We need to head out!"

She felt Benny's fingers slowly slip to her waist, digging into the fabric of her silk blouse and ensuring not even air could filter through their molded bodies. Another gravelly groan vibrated down her throat as he took their kiss deeper than she thought possible.

"Don't make me hose you down," the same voice tried again. This time waking up a few of Bethany's brain cells. She definitely didn't want to be hosed down.

With an animalistic growl, Benny pulled back. Releasing her lips but keeping their bodies fused together. His head snapping to the man beside them. He was dressed in the same uniform as Benny, scruffy brown hair sticking to his forehead as dark hair dotted his square jaw.

"If you ever interrupt me again while I'm kissing my woman, I'll stick that hose up your—"

Bethany's hand came up to his mouth. Stopping him from finishing that sentence and suppressing a smile as she did. "Nope! Just nope!"

His eyes came back to her then, softening as they locked onto her. "I'm defending your honor," he mumbled through her fingers.

"Really? Is that what you were doing?" Her lips quirked at that. "'Cause it sounded more like you were threatening a co-worker with cruel and unusual violence to me?"

"*Cruel and unusual* violence?" A dark eyebrow arched as she finally freed his lips.

"Well, threatening to shove uncomfortable objects into a man's orifices sounds pretty cruel to me. And *I'm hoping* it's not a common thing that goes down here in Woodvalley, otherwise I'll have to seriously reconsider setting up shop here."

"Hello?" Grumpy Fireman impatiently prompted. "We're out, Romeo. So, say goodbye to your girl. Get your shit. And let's go."

In no hurry to move, Benny continued to smile at her. "That's my friend Luke."

"Hi, Luke." She lifted her hand to wave at the man, her eyes not leaving Benny's as she did.

"Oh, for fucks sake," Luke grumbled.

The man was a laugh a minute.

"Come by my place tonight…after work?" Benny asked. "I'll be done by eight."

She nodded. Her attention going back to his lips as she felt the urge for one last taste. She didn't get a chance to take it though, not before Benny's head dipped again, claiming her lips and making her world tilt. Leaving her gasping, shaking, and more impatient for their night together than she thought possible.

***

This was dumb. Beyond stupid. A terrible, terrible idea.

The smoke fumes had clearly gone to her head. It was the only possible explanation as to why she was here, in her ex-boyfriend's kitchen, shamelessly flirting with him.

"What about this?" Bethany teased as she flitted from the toaster to the portable grill. A hand casually waving over the metal object.

Why are you like this?

The troll in her head may have been getting louder, but it had been fighting a losing battle all day.

"How many times, woman." He stalked toward her. Coming to a stop just a breath away, hands going to the counter on either side of her. Caging her in. "What part of *nothing* don't you understand?"

"You're seriously telling me there's *not one* single thing in this house that you've picked out yourself?" she challenged.

That easy smile turned wicked as he leaned closer. "I chose the bed." His voice dropped dangerously low. "You wanna come take a look?"

Strong hands went to her hips, his thumbs lazily stroking back and forth over denim.

"What are we doing?" Obviously high on ex-boyfriend fumes, she felt her voice shake.

His head drifted down until their foreheads touched. Ragged breaths landing on her lips, forcing her to squeeze her eyes shut. It was too much. She really was an idiot to think she could keep doing this. Accidentally sleeping with an ex once was one thing, but this? Was she seriously going to 'accidently' do it three times? Where was her self-control? Her dignity? Some sort of self-preservation instinct?

I think all that went out the window around the time you decided to hump his leg.

Shut up, brain! Can't some questions just be rhetorical?

Urgh.

"We're doing what feels right, NeNe." Goosebumps broke out on her forearms as those heavy breaths traveled up her jaw and landed on her ear. "We're doing what we're good at."

Okay. So it was true. Sex had technically been one thing they had always been good at. Even now, a decade on, she was woman enough to admit that Benjamin Tucker was the best she'd ever had. Still, it was a bitter pill to swallow. Especially as she had been about to marry a man who was sorely lacking in the *giving her orgasms* department.

If they stuck to sex, then really, this was just some basic self-care. Life was rough. Mind blowing orgasms are good for her wellbeing. Right?

Oh, now, you decide to stay quiet?

"Get out of your head, B," Benny drawled, knowing her far too well. "I told you, no more fucking around."

He had. He'd also gone on to state that she was his. And like the dumbass she was, she'd gone and told him that she was.

"I don't know what that means," she whispered into him, still not ready to open her eyes.

Benny pressed a kiss to the shell of her ear before

dragging those sinful lips back down the line of her jaw.

"*It means*, you want me, and I want you." Not helpful. "That we're not gonna fight it anymore." Another soft kiss. "No more running." He kissed her again, this time scraping her skin as he edged closer to her mouth. "That while we're doing this, *you're mine*." His lips then lightly brushed hers, making her shiver. "Mine to kiss. Mine to touch. Mine to *fuck*."

Goddamnit, stupid traitorous body. First the shiver, now she was panting.

Stop it!

Benny was her weakness. He knew exactly what she liked. What to say. How to touch her. She'd practically melted into him already. Her brain didn't stand a chance.

"Say it, NeNe. Tell me what I want to hear, and I'll give you what you need."

One big hand slipped from her hip, thick fingers trailing down until he reached her core. His thumb somehow found that magical spot and began teasing. Tracing circles. Going round and round and round. Getting harder and faster until the pressure that had been building inside her was too much. She was going to explode.

Don't say it. There's no going back if you say it.

It didn't matter they'd done this twice already. They both knew her giving him that trust again would change everything.

Benny's fingers curled until he was cupping her. His thumb continuing to drive her insane as his teeth tugged on her lower lip.

"Say it," he growled.

A whimper left her lips as his grip on her tightened. She couldn't think. It was getting hard to breathe.

"Okay," she panted. *Okay?* "You want me to say it?" She felt his chest vibrate. "*Fine*. Fine Benny, I'll say it."

The air charged. Her chest pounded. And her eyes opened. She wasn't surprised to find Benny's gaze on her. Dark with want. But she was surprised by how fiercely she wanted him back. It was all consuming. Unbearable. And really freaking scary.

No more fucking around.

"Do it," she breathed. "*Ruin me.*"

Benny's mouth took her in a singeing kiss. Taking her back in time to when he'd first allowed himself to lose control. Just the thought of it still made her body burn. It was another reminder that she'd not let go like this, either. Not since him.

Pulling back, her hands went to his face as she kept their mouths touching. "Make me feel it tomorrow," she pleaded, no longer caring about the consequences.

She felt a rip, it was either her jeans or her panties, both of which were being dragged down her thigh's moments later. Benny's sweats were next to be pulled down, leaving him just as bare. And ready.

She found her eyes darting down and there was a strong possibility she licked her lips. Jesus. This man. When she met his gaze again, his eyes were just as wild as she was feeling. Only getting wilder as he kept them on her. He didn't even glance down as he spit into his hand, using it to stroke himself.

"Turn around, B. Hands on the counter."

Sliding off the counter and down his muscled body, she wasn't just panting anymore; it was more like hyperventilating as he spun her and yanked her backward. She knew he didn't need to spit again as he teased her entrance, she was dripping, but she heard him do it anyway. Because that's how she liked it.

As he inched into her at a torturously slow pace, she knew deep down he'd already ruined her. Not today, not last week or the week before. He'd marked her a long time ago. And there was no scrubbing that mark off.

"Fuck," they both groaned as he finally filled her. He stayed there, not moving. Making her feel impossibly full. Her body arched, her palms were sweating, and her hips bucked. She needed more.

"Benny," she whined. "Please."

The man laughed. A dark chuckle. She was going to kill him.

Right after this orgasm?

Yes. Right after the orgasm she was practically guaranteed as Benny started to move again, this time with punishing thrusts that had already blown two brain cells.

Priorities.

CHAPTER TWELVE

Benny was so fucked.

It seemed like a good idea in his head. They clearly couldn't keep their hands off each other so why fight it? But now he was second guessing himself. He was already too far gone.

You're an idiot.

The sound of his alarm going off was just another reminder he was in over his head.

Reaching for his phone, he quickly put an end to the ringing. His gaze going back to the beautiful woman on his chest who was now stirring.

Last night, they'd not just crossed a line, they'd taken a match to it and scorched the fucking earth.

Ruin me.

He was the ruined one. That phrase was what she'd asked the first time he'd ever lost control with her. Taking her hard. Dirty. All the while whispering filthy things in her ear. To this day she was still the only woman he'd trusted to let go with. Which was unsurprising, seeing as she'd been his one and only relationship. One-night stands weren't exactly the time to surprise someone with dominant demands and rough hands. Not that he wanted to do that with a stranger, either.

It wasn't just the mind-blowing sex that had sparked his

inevitable ruin, though. It was the whole night. And the complete lack of boundaries enforced to protect his heart. They cooked. They laughed. They kissed. And he held her all night long. Now this. His hand lifted, his fingers going straight to the silky strands of dark hair dusted over his chest.

"Hey," Bethany's head lifted, sleepy eyes meeting his. "What time is it?"

She made no attempt to move. To untangle her legs from his. To remove the hand currently resting on his stomach. Or shift the naked curves plastered against his side.

"Seven, baby." His sleep worn voice croaked. "You at the clinic today?"

Clearly a sucker for punishment, he dropped a soft kiss to her forehead. Lapping up the lazy smile she gave him as his chest squeezed.

"Yeah." She dropped her head again. "I should get up or I'm going to be late."

Again, she made no attempt to move. Not that he wanted to, either. In fact, he wanted something else entirely.

Are you freaking serious?

He silently continued to fight a losing battle. He was already fucked. Already ruined. It's not like he could take anything they'd done back. It was too late.

So, you want to fall further down the rabbit hole? Guarantee your heart isn't just shattered the next time she leaves you, but burnt to ash as well.

Apparently, he did. Because before he had a chance to overthink it more, he was flipping them both over until he hovered above Bethany. Positioning himself between her legs as he stared down into perfection.

"We're both gonna be late, B," he declared.

"We are?" She arched a delicate brow in question.

Instead of answering, he realigned himself until he was resting against her core. One slow drag later and his dick was pressing against that sensitive spot that never failed to make his girl moan.

Your girl?

Shut up.

He ground down. Harder this time. A devilish smile tipping his lips as Bethany mewed. Followed by a sharp curse.

"I can't be late," she meekly protested as her head arched into the pillow.

Slowly, he dragged his length again. This time he used his hand to position himself at her entrance. Letting the tip tease her until slick heat soaked his skin. Making him want to groan.

"So, you don't want to be a good girl and spread those legs for me, baby?" He pressed again.

Her hips were bucking, chasing friction. "Please," she moaned.

"Please what, NeNe?" He felt his voice scrape as his head dipped and his lips went to hers. "Please take what's mine?"

"Yes," she gulped. "Take it. It's yours. *I'm yours.*"

Damn fucking right she is.

***

Three days had passed since Bethany had woken up in his bed, and while he was happy that he was no longer being ghosted, he wasn't exactly thrilled that the next time they were going to see each other was at the Thursday night support group. Not only did they have an audience, but Benny was also at his most vulnerable. Hence, the current bouncing of his knee.

"You, okay?" his mom whispered as she leaned into him.

They'd both taken their seats in the circle, tonight's meeting just minutes away from starting.

"Yeah. All good," he grunted, eyes returning to the front door.

Lies.

So many lies. He'd been dodging questions all week after his very public kiss with Bethany. Not only from his mom, but the whole damn town.

Catherine clapped, bringing all their attention to the petite older woman. "Who'd like to kick us off today?"

His stomach dropped as all eyes turned in his direction. He didn't need to look to know his mother's hand was raised.

Perfect.

"Please, go ahead, Gloria." Catherine's soothing tone did nothing to ease his churning insides.

The sudden ring of the shop bell was a welcome distraction as his head snapped up. Bethany. His heartbeat kicked up, and his lips twitched as he watched her make her way toward the circle with all the exaggerated grace of a cartoon burglar. In heels.

Sliding into the empty seat next to Catherine, their eyes locked immediately as she mouthed a shy "Hi." But she didn't wait for him to return the greeting, her gaze went straight to his mother as she continued to share.

Benny kept his eyes on Bethany throughout. Absorbing every emotion that flickered across her pretty face. She didn't hide the sadness causing tears to pool. The pain thickening her swallows. Or the pride making her nostrils flare. Somehow, just looking at her, made his mother's words hurt less. And when her eyes met his again, he knew what he had to do.

***

Two hours later, they were back at Benny's. But they'd yet to talk.

After the session, Bethany had been pulled over by a few members. Answering their questions dutifully and handing out her contact information. Long after he'd said his goodbyes to his mother, she'd still been deep in conversation. Feeling slightly creepy watching her for so long, he'd given up, shooting off a text for her to meet him back at his house when she was done, before slinking out.

Now, she was here. In his living room, fiddling with the label of the beer bottle she held, submerged in his overly stuffed cream couch.

"I—" Bethany started at the same time as Benny said, "We should—"

Tight smiles tugged on both their lips, but it was Bethany who gestured for him to go first.

Clearing his throat, he did. "I was gonna say we should talk about it. What happened."

He didn't elaborate. She knew. They'd both shied away from the subject ever since that first meeting. It was time to change that.

Bethany nodded, taking a swig of her beer before asking the question he knew was coming. "Why didn't you say anything?"

He didn't have a good answer. Not really. While he hadn't planned on telling her, it didn't mean he never regretted it.

Blowing out a long breath, his hand rubbed the back of his neck. "I...I knew you'd want to stay, B. And I couldn't do that to you. I was already the reason you deferred a year, waiting for me to get my shit together and figure out what I wanted to do with my life. I just...I couldn't stand the idea of holding you back any longer."

His head may have been fucked at the time, but he still loved her. So fucking much. Enough to put her first. And that's what he thought he was doing.

Bethany's head shook. "No."

"No?" he asked when she didn't elaborate.

"No. That's not what we had. That's not what we were." His chest squeezed at all the pain she was making no attempt to cover. "We told each other everything, Benny. *Everything*. Try again."

What was he supposed to say to that?

Try again, maybe?

Shit. He let his hand scrub over his face. Letting the silence between them grow thicker as his mind raced.

"I was scared." His voice was as raw as the admission.

It may not be an explanation, but it was the truth.

Bethany's eyes were on him. Searching. He could practically see her holding her breath as she waited patiently for him to go on. So he did.

"There were so many unknowns. What stage the cancer was. If it had spread. What her treatment options would be." He felt exposed as she stared into him. "I thought she was going to fucking die."

While her features softened, the heaviness in the air clung to his lungs.

"I should have told you. You were my person and fuck...I needed you. I did. I know that." He let out a heavy sigh. "But I just...I was barely surviving. I was on autopilot. Trying my best to get through every day without falling apart."

"So, us breaking up...*me*. I was one less thing in your life for you to worry about?" He watched her gaze drop back to the bottle label as her throat bobbed.

"No. Jesus. No, B. No fucking way." How could she even think that? "Are you seriously trying to tell me you'd have gone off to school after I told you what was going on with my mom?"

He knew the answer. They both did. She didn't have to say it. Which is why when their eyes met again, he continued.

"I thought I was doing the right thing. Letting you go. Knowing you were doing what you were supposed to be doing...it was the only thing that kept me sane. Made losing you worth it."

Damnit. It wasn't worth it though, was it? Allowing his head to fall into his hands he tried to catch his breath. Memories coming thick and fast. He tried so hard to be strong for his mom, but between appointments, he unraveled. Spiraled. He smoked too much. Drank more than was healthy. Spent way too much time alone. His world was upside down and the one person he wanted to talk about it with—he'd pushed away. God only knows what would have happened to him if he hadn't joined the fire department when he did. It saved him. Gave him focus. A purpose. And best of all, something else to think about.

He faintly heard Bethany sink into the cushions next to him. Her soft hands wrapping around his face, coaxing his gaze to hers. "Hey. You're right."

"I am?"

"I would have stayed." Her words were quiet but no less impactful. "No matter how hard you tried to convince me not to, *I would have stayed*." Benny's knuckles went to her cheek, where he trailed them over the apple and down to her jaw. "I'm really fucking stubborn."

"Yeah, you are." He felt his lips tip up as he dragged his knuckles back up over silky skin. "My girl is stubborn as hell."

And she *was* his girl. Time hadn't changed that. He knew that now. All time had done was make him impatient. He was sick of waiting. Ten damn years. Waiting for her to return to Woodvalley, even just for a visit. Hoping she'd call, enough that he'd never changed his number. And, of course, avoiding any kind of relationship because no one was *her*.

Jesus Christ I'm pathetic.

"Okay," she said out of nowhere.

"Okay?" That wasn't what he was expecting. Was she giving him an out?

Instead of expanding, she leaned into him. A soft kiss grazing his lips as he let his eyes flutter closed. He didn't know how much he needed her touch until just then. When she went to pull back, he held on. One hand going to her neck, the other to her hip as he tugged her closer. His mouth covering hers again. His tongue teasing the seam until she parted for him.

It was too easy to pick up where they'd left off. Physically that is. His attraction to Bethany, the chemistry they shared—he'd never been able to get lost in anyone the way he did with her. Emotionally though, they had some catching up to do. And addressing how they ended up where they were now wasn't the only thing he wanted to discuss tonight. Which was why he released her. Not letting her get too far as his hands remained in place. His thumb gently stroking the pulse point at her neck.

"I know you don't want to talk about what's going on between us, but I think we need to."

A heavy breath hit his lips, as she looked away. "Can't we just live in this bubble a little longer?"

"Baby, trust me when I say that's all I wanna do. But after what happened on the highway, and the rumors still swirling from the wedding…well, people apparently have questions. And opinions. A whole hell of a lot of them."

Bethany may be able to dodge the locals while working up in Goldacre, but he didn't have that luxury.

"Let me guess, Mrs. Molly?" She gave him a small smile. One he matched before replying.

"Mrs. Molly, my friends, my mother…Darla from the Tipsy Cow, who said and I quote 'don't fuck it up this time, pretty boy'."

Bethany's smile only grew, that familiar twinkle reaching her eyes that he felt all the way in his gut. "*Pretty boy?*" she teased.

Benny shrugged. "What can I say, I'm pretty. No need to hate."

"You're pretty something…" The smack to his chest made his hands drop. But they didn't stay down for long before he captured her waist and hauled her onto his lap.

"So…" He guided her down until his forehead rested against hers. "You ready to put a label on this, NeNe?"

"Ummm…no. Absolutely not." Why did that sting so much? "It's not even been a month since I ran out on my wedding, Benny. Doug is…fuck. Doug doesn't deserve this. Me rubbing whatever this is in his face."

Right. Doug. Like he could forget she was about to marry another man.

"No offence, B, but what did you think was going to happen when you kissed me last week? You don't think that was rubbing 'whatever this is' in his face?"

"I agreed to meet with him."

"What?" His whole body stiffened.

"For coffee, this weekend. I need to…I don't know…I just…he deserves a conversation, you know?"

Benny knew, he really did. They were supposed to be married. He got it. The need for closure. But that didn't mean he had to like it. Or that his stomach wasn't bottoming out at the thought of it. So instead of voicing all the jealous, possessive and damn right crazy demands that had suddenly infiltrated his thoughts, he stayed quiet.

"Look, I'm not saying we should hide what's happening with us…but I really don't want to go out of my way to advertise it, either. I know I messed up by kissing you in front of people. But right now, I need to be respectful."

"Why did you?"

"Why did I what?"

"Why did you kiss me in front of everyone?"

Benny's pulse pounded as he waited for her answer. Lost in her deep green eyes as she stared into him.

"I couldn't not kiss you, Benny," she whispered.

And just like that, not kissing Bethany Mayer right now, in his living room, was no longer an option, either.

ISOBEL REED

CHAPTER THIRTEEN

"You didn't think to mention you didn't love me—before our fucking wedding?"

Bethany flinched at Doug's harsh words. When she'd agreed to meet him at Molly's Diner, naively, she didn't realize it would be so hard.

Unable to keep staring at the pain she was responsible for; her gaze dropped to the coffee she had yet to touch.

"I don't know when it happened," she confessed. "Between the wedding and the move, everything...I don't know. I didn't have a chance to breathe let alone think."

"That's seriously your excuse—you didn't have time to tell me you stopped loving me?" Doug barked, making her flinch again, this time her eyes squeezed shut.

There was no excuse. No good explanation. She knew that. He did, too. She wished she could go back and do things differently; she really did.

"When did you start fucking him?" That had her eyes and mouth opening as her head snapped up. "Was it before or after we moved here?"

She felt her eyes bug out. "Nothing happened with Benny until after we broke up, Doug. I swear. I wouldn't do that to you."

A humorless laugh left his lips. "Right. 'Cause you're all about respect, aren't you, Beth? It's not like you'd spend our wedding night at your ex-boyfriend's house, is it…oh wait!"

Asshole.

Bethany looked at the man before her. Really looked. Back when they'd met, she thought he was handsome. Sophisticated. And out of her league. He always dressed well, kept himself cleanly shaved, while his short brown hair maintained a neat and tidy style with weekly visits to the barber. He was tall, in good shape and had all the charm you'd expect from a private wealth manager who regularly wooed new clients.

He was everything she thought she wanted. But sitting before him now, she wondered if she ever really knew him. Let alone loved him. She certainly hadn't seen this side of him before. It made her wonder if all the feelings she had were even real. Or was she just doing and saying what she thought she should be doing and saying. She wasn't about to tell him that though, she was already on her way to hell, she didn't need an express ticket.

"Nothing happened that night," she reiterated.

"So, when did it happen then?" His thick brow lifted in challenge.

Okay. So the truth wasn't exactly going to make her look much better. Or feel it. But anything was better than the day of the wedding, right?

Yeah, tell Lucifer that when he's warming up those pokers, sister.

"We kissed about a week after the wedding. Just kissed." Her eyes went back to the brown liquid below her.

Another sharp, not very funny laugh escaped Doug. "You're a piece of work, Beth. I guess I should be happy I didn't fucking marry you."

I mean, I am.

Shush. Hell, remember!

She felt bad. Guilty. But that didn't mean she wasn't also relieved. Happy even, that they were over. *This* was over.

"I just wished I'd worked out what a whore you were before I moved to this backward-ass town of yours, it could have saved me a fuck-load of time and money." Doug was pushing up from his seat and throwing his napkin on the steel tabletop a moment later.

Don't.

She should let him leave. Let it go. She'd already humiliated him. And she was going to leave it, she really was. But then he went and said, "Oh, and just so you know, I lied—yes you *have* put on weight. And no, it's not fucking sexy."

Oh, no he didn't.

"Yeah?" It was her turn to rise from her chair. Her voice louder than it should be as she pointed her finger his way. "Well, I lied, too. Size *does* matter, asshole! Especially when you have no idea what to do with it!"

It was petty. She was petty. But he fucking started it.

"Whore!" he yelled.

"Dick!" she called back. "Or should that be *microdick?*"

He was in her face a second later. Her heart going a mile a minute as she got a glimpse of the hate filling his eyes.

"Fuck you, Beth. You're a shit lay. And once your ex is done pity-fucking you, you're going to spend the rest of your life alone. Regretting letting go of the only man who was able to stand you."

Yeah. He hated her alright. She didn't even have a comeback for that. Not when he'd stolen all the oxygen from her lungs with that slap in the face.

"Get out!" Bethany's eyes went to Lucy, who was somehow in Doug's face now. "Take your dumb face and get out of this diner before this pie and I choose violence."

Doug was storming out before she'd even had a chance to catch her breath. She faintly heard him cursing while other diners applauded his exit as she slumped back into her chair. Her elbows hitting the table as her head fell into her hands.

Well, that was humiliating.

This was not how today was supposed to go. It was supposed to be civilized. It was supposed to be a conversation. Not a shouting match. Not a fight. And when did her best friend grow such big balls? She'd never so much as heard Lucy raise her voice above a normal level before.

"You, okay?" Lucy asked.

"No." Bethany sighed; her face still buried. "Is everyone looking at me?"

"Um, do you want the truth, or do you want me to lie?"

That pulled out one of her own humorless laughs. "Lie."

"Ah, okay, then. Denial it is. In that case, no one is looking. No one heard any of that. And Betty definitely did not take a picture to include in the town blog."

Bethany let out a pained groan. "Fuck my fucking life."

It just kept getting better and better.

"You look pretty today, though," Lucy went on. "You're having a good hair day."

Bethany uncovered her face and gave her friend a sad smile. "Is that another lie?"

Lucy shook her head. "No. And don't listen to a word that jerk nugget said. You're beautiful and kind and smart and anyone would be lucky to be with you."

"*Jerk nugget?*" Her smile got bigger.

Lucy shrugged, white teeth peeking out as her smile widened. "Just calling it like I see it. Come on, I'll buy you some pie."

Thank God for good friends. And pie.

***

Bethany was relieved to be among friendly faces. Yesterday was brutal. So much so, she'd blown Benny off and gone back to Lucy's to lick her wounds and devour a tub of ice cream, two packs of Cheetos and a frozen pizza.

But today was a new day. And she was determined to enjoy it. It's why she'd said yes to a barbecue with Benny's friends. She was also feeling especially proud that she'd managed to convince Lucy to come, claiming emotional support needs.

They were currently in Zach and Libby's yard. Sipping

on cold beers and stuffing their faces with burgers.

Benny was looking all manly in his fire department tee and jeans, flipping burgers on the grill while Bethany and Lucy were stuffing their faces, off to the side.

"Yes!" Cat shouted, bringing their attention to the dark-haired woman now waving her phone as she sauntered toward Libby. "Jack's flying over to meet little bean. And he's going to stay a while—help out. Booked time off and everything!"

"Who's Jack?" Bethany discreetly whispered to Lucy.

"Cat's brother." Her friend gulped. Loud enough to have Bethany sneaking a peek at her. Her usual pale skin taking on a pinker shade.

"Do we *like* Jack?"

"What?" Lucy snapped.

Hmm. Touchy subject.

"I'm just asking, do we *like* Jack? Do we *know* Jack? Is there a reason every time I mention *Jack*, that you seem to go a darker shade of red?"

"I hate you." Lucy glared.

"You love me." Bethany grinned. "And someone called Jack, apparently."

That comment earned her a swat to the arm. Worth it. She was suddenly looking forward to meeting this Jack guy.

She didn't get to interrogate Lucy any further because the next thing she knew, Benny's arms were wrapping around her waist. And with one tug, her back was plastered against his hard chest. His lips ghosting down her neck as he murmured, "I missed you," along her sensitive skin.

"You were gone five minutes," she pointed out, slightly breathier than normal. "And you were like two yards away."

Leaning into him, she embraced the goosebumps as he nipped at the spot under her ear. "What can I say? Even two yards is too far, baby."

"Annnd...I'm getting another drink." She could practically hear Lucy's eyes roll before her friend disappeared back inside the house.

Benny and Bethany remained wrapped in each other for a while. His nose and lips tracing the line along her neck as she breathed in fresh pine. She felt at peace for the first time in a long time. Sure, there were plenty of things she could overthink. And a ridiculous number of recent decisions she should seek professional help for. But self-flagellation wasn't on today's agenda. Doug's dressing down was enough punishment for this weekend.

She let a satisfied sigh escape as Benny trailed soft kisses across her shoulder. Damnit, she could get used to this.

"You ready to label this now, B?" Amusement laced his tone as more kisses peppered the skin between her tank top and neckline.

"Nope." She smiled, popping the "p."

He'd been asking every day since the last support group and her answer was always the same. Because of the sickos that they were, it had now become a running joke. And would remain one while she continued to bask in the comfort of denial.

"Hey, Bethany," Libby greeted as she approached them. "You think I could steal you away from Benny for a minute?"

While Libby's smile was friendly, Bethany could tell she was nervous as she twiddled with the long brown waves that she'd gathered over one shoulder.

"Yeah, of course." Bethany untangled herself, and with a quick twist of her neck, she pecked Benny's lips before following Libby inside.

The back door led them through the kitchen where Lucy and Rachel sat at the small wooden table, giggling between sips of beer. With a quick wave to her friend, she continued through the giant arch and into the living room where Libby gestured for her to sit.

"You and Benny seem happy," she noted, exhaling softly as she joined her on the bouncy couch.

"Oh, God, is this another warning not to break his heart—'cause you should know that Cat and Rachel already beat you to it."

Libby's sing-song laugh echoed around the room as her hand waved her off. "God, no! Not at all!"

Bethany could see it now. Her husband Zach always called her "princess." And with those wide Disney-like eyes, long thick hair and hourglass figure, it didn't take a genius to figure out why. She was also super sweet. Even now, as she looked at Bethany, unsure, and chewed on painted pink lips.

"I, uh, I actually wanted your professional opinion on something, if you don't mind?"

Was it wrong that she was so relieved to hear that? Professional she could do. It was her default. And the idea of easing the nerves radiating off the woman before her was something she definitely wanted to do.

"Of course. Shoot."

"So. Um. Zach and I have been trying to, you know, start a family." Bethany simply nodded, urging her to continue. "Well, we've been trying for a while now and it's got to the point where I think it's me. I think there's something wrong with me." Watery eyes flicked from her to the carpet. "Zach got tested and all is good there, so it must be me, right?"

Bethany scooched nearer, her hand going to Libby's arm. "That's not necessarily true and even if it turns out to be the case, there's usually different options or things you can do to help you to conceive. Do you mind if I ask you a couple of questions?"

Libby gave her a gentle nod.

"Okay, do you mind me asking how long you've been trying and if you're having regular menstrual cycles?"

"A year. And yes. I've always been regular." She was back to chewing her lip.

"Any gynecological issues or previous pregnancies in the past?" Libby shook her head. "And any other health conditions or medication that you're currently taking?" Another head shake.

Okay. This was good news.

"Have you been tracking your ovulation at all?"

"No, I mean, there's not many days when we don't, well, you know." Bethany couldn't help but let out a short laugh as she watched Libby turn an adorable shade of pink.

"Okay." She cleared her throat, attempting to put on her best serious doctor face. "Well, I'm not super concerned."

"You're not?" There was that hope.

"No, Libby. Most people don't realize that it can take couples up to two years to conceive naturally. So, before I recommend any sort of invasive fertility tests for you, I'd like you to try out a few things for me—how does that sound?"

"Like I love you and want to kiss you." She excitedly bounced. Her contagious smile was enough to penetrate Bethany's super serious doctor face.

"Well, hold on to that sentiment while I tell you to cut out the caffeine and alcohol for the next few months." As expected, the woman's face dropped. "You need to make sure you're eating well and getting enough sleep. Stress levels also need to be managed accordingly, and you need to stay active—and yes, sex totally counts." The smile returned at that. "And I want you to track your ovulation every month. Your fertile window starts around five days before you ovulate so around this window try to have sex as often as possible to increase your chances. If we don't see any results, we can review again in three months. Any questions?"

Instead of questions, Libby launched herself at her. Her arms flung around Bethany in a heartfelt hug. One she returned without thinking twice.

"Thank you," she whispered into the crook of Bethany's neck. "Thank you so much."

This was why she loved her job. She wanted to help people. It made her so fucking happy. The woman in her arms a reminder of what exactly she came here to achieve and why. Woodvalley needed a doctor and goddamnit, she was going to give them one.

CHAPTER FOURTEEN

Over the past few weeks, Benny and Bethany had settled into a couple-like routine. They spent every night he wasn't on shift together at his house. Talking, cooking, watching the terrible reality shows she liked, and getting busy on every surface. Once a week, they'd hang out with his friends, usually dragging Lucy along, too. It felt good. Easy. Like this was what his life was supposed to look like. And while she still refused to label what they were doing, it was pretty obvious to him and the rest of the town what was going on.

He did want that label, though. Badly. But he didn't push for it. He was too much of a coward, too afraid of losing her again if he did.

"Can I open my eyes yet?" Bethany asked.

"So impatient," he tutted, guiding her through the double doors.

Bringing her to a stop in the doorway, he felt the need to brace before giving her the go ahead. "Okay. Now. Now you can open them."

The afternoon light filtered in from the front windows, catching the dust swirl in the air. At first glance, the space wasn't anything special. A long-forgotten hardware store, a few doors down from the fire station. But as soon as Benny had seen it, he'd felt it. He just hoped Bethany felt it, too.

Watching her take a tentative step into the room, he

stayed where he was, his hands going into his jean pockets as he propped himself up against the doorframe. The floorboards groaned as she took another step, then another. Her gaze first darting to the walls where old tool shelves had left their outlines and then up to the exposed beams decorating the high ceilings. A small smile tilted her lips as her fingers trailed over the scuffed wooden counter. And when she came to one of the rooms off to the side, she audibly inhaled.

She feels it.

Bethany's eyes flung to him, her whole body twisting to face him. He didn't wait for her to speak before saying, "You can see it, yeah?"

"How? When?" She shook her head. "Why?"

Okay, so he had to admit that this was a little out of the blue. They'd only spoken once about her wanting to maybe, possibly, open a clinic in Woodvalley when she was done with her residency next year. Perhaps too excited by the prospect, he'd got carried away with the idea.

"One of the guys at the station was talking about this rejuvenation project the town council have put forward. There are all these new incentives to try and get some of the empty shop fronts filled. And I thought about this place and I just…I don't know. I just thought of you. Of your practice. The space has so much potential. You could get a really good deal on the lease and take your time getting it ready, setting it up like you want it. Me and some of the guys could work on it, too, in our spare time, seeing as it's down the road from the station." When she remained silent, his hand went to his neck where he began to rub. Suddenly, he felt embarrassed. It was presumptuous of him to assume she was even staying in town. He'd overstepped.

At that thought, his eyes hit the scratched floor.

Learn some fucking boundaries, man.

He was too busy berating himself to hear Bethany approach, and it wasn't until her fingers were under his chin, pushing his face up to meet hers that he felt like he could breathe again.

"I love it, Benny," she beamed. "It's perfect."

"Yeah?" He felt a hopeful smile stretch all the way to his ears.

"Yeah." Her voice was soft as her lips brushed his in a kiss infused with gratitude. She rested her forehead against his, her breath warm against his skin. "Thank you for thinking of me," she murmured, her fingers curling lightly in his shirt. "Thank you for volunteering to help." Another kiss followed, deeper, slower, leaving his heart to stumble over itself. "And thank you," she whispered, eyes glittering. "For being exactly who you are."

Well, fuck me. Does this mean she's staying?

Like the coward he was, he didn't ask. Even though he was dying to know what she meant. If she was going to take the space. If she was going to stay here, in Woodvalley, with him. *Forever.* Instead, he took her hand and led her into the first room off to the side.

Clearing his throat, he went on. "Both rooms are the same size, but this one has a storage space off to the side that you could use for equipment, medication, stuff like that."

He didn't need to look to know she was grinning as she looped her arm around his waist and leaned into him. "I just can't believe what good condition everything is in. I mean, I remember this place closing when we were teenagers and it doesn't look like anyone has been here since then."

They hadn't.

"There will be some building work, we'll need to put in toilets, maybe a small kitchen area…there's a stock room out back that I think could work. Everything else, though, will be superficial. A lick of paint, polish up the floors, furniture, that kind of thing." Feeling her eyes on him, he dipped his head to look at her. "What?"

"*We?*" She smiled.

He drew in a breath. "Yeah, NeNe, *we*. If you let me, I want to help. You don't have to do anything alone anymore." *Or ever.*

He held her stare, her expression going from teasing to thoughtful as she searched his eyes. When was she going to get it? He wanted her. He wanted this.

"Okay." She gulped. "Tell me more about these incentives."

And just like that, it wasn't just his face lighting up, it was his heart, too.

***

"Sweet, baby Jesus, this is sooo fucking good."

Benny shifted again under the wooden bench, trying his hardest to discreetly adjust himself. Bethany's breathy whimpers were officially torturing him. His body didn't seem to care that they were surrounded by friends. Or that they were enjoying a delicious meal at the Evans ranch's new farm to table restaurant. He wanted her. Right here, right now. So, he did what any mature adult who found themselves in the same situation would do—he tortured her right back.

Leaning in close, he let his lips brush the shell of her ear. "You keep teasing me with those pretty little moans, baby, and I'm dragging you the fuck out of here." His voice was low and ragged as he felt her breathing hitch. "I'll have you on your knees before the door even closes. Taking every inch like a good girl."

She bit down on her lower lip, a slow smile curling at the edges as her gaze remained on the plate of food in front of her. "Is that a promise or a threat?" she whispered.

"Both," he said before nipping her lobe.

His hand went to her clenched thighs next where he pulled them apart. His fingers moving slowly, lazily, gliding up smooth, creamy skin until they reached the hem of her dress. That was where he paused, knuckles brushing the soft underside of her thigh. Taking pleasure in the needy whimper she let slip as she attempted to press her legs back together.

Benny kept her open for him. Savoring every tremble as his fingers inched higher. Close enough to feel the heat radiating from her. The higher he went, the more he started to question himself. One gentle swipe of damp panties and he had to suppress a groan. Now he was the one being tortured all over again.

"You're so fucking wet." His mouth was hovering over her ear again. His voice strained. "Is that all for me, NeNe?"

"Yes." He watched her chest heave.

Fuck me.

This time, his knuckles dragged over the thin, damp fabric covering her. "Tell me what's got you soaked, baby." He increased the pressure in his touch ever so slightly, enough to feel her shake. "Is it the thought of me punishing that pretty little mouth of yours?" Bethany's breathing picked up again. "Or is it knowing what a mess you're going to make when you're done begging?"

He couldn't help but smile as a few choice curse words slipped from her pouty lips. But it was when she abruptly stood that had him grinning like a damn cheshire cat.

"Right. We're going," she announced to the group. Her gaze landing on Riley, Wade's girlfriend and tonight's chef, when she declared, "Dinner was fucking delicious, thank you." He then found himself being tugged up from his seat. "I just remembered that I have a clinical audit I need to complete for my supervisor and it's due tomorrow."

Benny stifled a laugh as his friends looked confused and slightly amused by the abrupt exit.

"Yep." Benny's smug grin was still going strong. "We're gonna go audit the fuck outta that paperwork. Catch y'all later."

He didn't miss his friend's snickers, but it was only when they were safely out the door and nearing his truck that he let his laugh break free.

"Jesus Christ, woman," he said, still vibrating, almost breathless from holding it in. "If I'd have known you were this damn horny, I wouldn't have even let you leave the house—I wouldn't have even let you put clothes on."

Bethany gave his chest a playful smack, but the grin on her face said she was anything but sorry. Which was good because nor was he.

"Come on, NeNe. We've got places to be and…messes to be made." He shot her a wink, her giggles filling the night sky.

Grabbing her hand, he quickly picked up speed and tugged her toward their ride.

Tonight was about to get better.

CHAPTER FIFTEEN

"So?" Lucy, the queen of patience, was finally cracking at Bethany's silence.

She'd brought her best friend to the space that could potentially be her new practice an hour ago. At first, Bethany had been excited, ordering them takeout as she rambled on about what could go where. But as they both sat cross-legged in the middle of the shop floor, eating pizza, excitement had morphed into crippling fear.

"What's going on in that completely unhinged brain of yours?" Lucy calmly asked, picking up another slice from the open box between them.

"I should do this...tell me I should do this." She sounded desperate even to her own ears, so she wasn't surprised to see Lucy's baby blues widen.

"You've literally just spent an hour talking about all the things you're going to do to this place..."

"It's a big commitment." Bethany's teeth dug into her lower lip. "I've recently discovered I'm not great at those."

She watched Lucy's eyes roll. "You're being dramatic." Bethany shot her an unimpressed glare, that clearly didn't indicate she should elaborate. One her friend chose to ignore. "Okay, let me get this straight. You make the *right* decision to not go ahead and marry a man you're not in love with...and now you're questioning whether you're cut out for commitment?" Yes. Exactly. She was glad they were on the same page.

An exasperated sigh left Lucy's lips before she continued. "I'm seriously questioning the intelligence of everyone in the medical field right now. Do they teach you to be this dumb at college?"

"Um, rude!" Bethany hurled her crust, aiming right for her so-called friend's forehead.

"B, I can't believe you need me to say this to you, but I guess I don't have a choice." Lucy's hand slowly dragged down her face in what looked more like frustration than anything else. "You're the most committed person I know. Do I need to remind you that you've spent a decade training to be a doctor?"

She didn't need a reminder of that. She'd worked her ass off. A four-year undergraduate degree, four-years of medical school and now she was in her third and final year of her residency in family medicine. She was so close she could taste it.

"Fine," she huffed. "But what about Woodvalley...what about me staying here...setting up shop. If I do this, if I take this lease, there's no turning back."

Lucy eyed her thoughtfully for a moment. "You're talking about, Benny." She correctly guessed. "You've already committed to Woodvalley. You did that the moment you moved back with Doug the Douche. The only reason you'd have second thoughts is...Benny."

It was true. The decision to move back. Start a life here. Build her own practice. That was made long before she stepped back into town.

"Oh, God," she moaned into her hands which were now over her face. "I'm *that* woman. I *hate* that woman." She faintly heard her friend laughing at her pain. "The one who's going to let some stupid guy determine what she does or doesn't do with her life."

She was pathetic.

"So don't be that woman, B," Lucy said between bites

of pizza. "Do this for you. Fuck what happens with Benny. This is yours. This is what you've always wanted. Don't let anyone take that away from you. Sign the lease and woman up."

Her hands immediately dropped, eyes widening at her friend as her mouth hung open in disbelief.

"What?" Lucy fidgeted under her stare, still chewing.

"Did you just say *fuck?*" Bethany didn't bother hiding the amusement in her voice. Her best friend had just cursed. For the first time ever.

She was treated to the most aggressive eye roll she'd ever witnessed and then it was her turn to take a pizza crust to the head.

Worth it.

***

Deep breaths. You've got this.

As her gaze landed on the hand Benny was holding, she knew she was lying to herself.

"B, it's okay," he soothed. "It's not going to be as bad as you think."

She let out a very unladylike snort as she used her free hand to press the doorbell. It was definitely going to be as bad as she thought. Her parents were still pissed. Every time she'd called over the past two months, they'd blown her off, usually with the vague excuse of having to be somewhere that wasn't on the phone with her.

Benny was here for moral support. She still wasn't ready to label what they were doing, which is why when her mother swung the door open, she let go of his hand.

Her mom immediately frowned. *Excellent. Off to a great start.* Her mother smoothed an imaginary strand of straight dark hair and blanked her expression.

Typical.

"Bethany." Was her greeting. "What are you doing here?"

She wasn't a fan of the term "ambush," nevertheless that was exactly what she was doing. This was getting silly. Her parents needed to grow up and deal with her runaway bride town status.

"We need to talk, Mom. Is Dad here?"

Her mother's brow furrowed, her blue eyes darting between Bethany and Benny.

She cleared her throat. "Yes. Yes, he is. Come on in." She turned to Benny then and greeted him with a stern nod. "Benjamin."

"Mrs. Mayer." He gave her his signature easy smile and as they both stepped over the threshold, Benny's hand found Bethany's again. "It's good to see you."

Her mother didn't miss the hand holding, sending a disapproving glare at Bethany. Before giving them both a view of the back of her expensive looking fitted dress.

Just breathe.

Led through the bright white hallway, they stepped into the equally white kitchen located at the back of the house. As always, it was pristine, looking more like a magazine spread than a family home.

Her mother came to a stop at the marble island. "We weren't expecting company, so we don't have much in, but I can get you a coffee, soda, water?"

Bethany fought the urge to scoff. Their one and only child could hardly be considered 'company', but this was typical of her mother. Formal was the only way she knew how to be. With how she acted, you'd think they were members of high society, not living in a small town in Wyoming.

After both of them requested coffee, her mother went about making it, calling out to Bethany's father as she did. Bethany just stood there, like an idiot. She was suddenly glad Benny had insisted on coming. This all felt awkward. The silence deafening.

Benny seemed to read her mind. Giving her hand a reassuring squeeze. And with a gentle tug, he led them to the marble island, letting go of her to pull out a cream bar stool each. She sat woodenly on the chair chewing her lip while Benny made friendly small talk with her mother. She let herself zone out, no desire to discuss the balmy June weather.

Her nerves hadn't subsided though, she was still biting down on her lip when her father joined them. Thankfully, he gave them a much warmer reception, planting a kiss on Bethany's forehead and giving Benny a friendly pat on the back.

Once they were all seated, coffee in hand, Bethany was the one to kick things off, before she changed her mind.

"I know you're mad about the wedding, but I need you to forgive me," she rushed out. "I know it was expensive and yes, I should have called it off earlier, but I honestly thought I was just getting cold feet. Everyone is always talking about cold feet, so when I started feeling sick at the idea of marrying Doug, I kept thinking...okay, this is what everyone talks about...my feet are cold. But they were freezing, you know?" Benny's hand went to her thigh where he let his thumb stroke back and forth in a soothing motion. She knew she was rambling, but she couldn't stop. "*Sooo* freaking cold. Like *frostbite* cold. *Amputation* cold. But everyone was just so excited. *You. Doug.* Lucy kept going on about all the girl's nights we were gonna have...and I'd already transferred my residency...and the apartment—"

"Bethy," her dad cut her off. "It's okay. Take a breath." His kind green eyes held her in place. "We're not mad at you."

"You're not?" Then what was with the silent treatment.

One glance at her mom's face told a different story. But her father kept going.

"We just wanted to give you some space," her dad said softly. "After everything that happened...for you to make a decision like that and feel like you couldn't come to us— well, we thought maybe you just needed some time to process it all, without any pressure. And we trusted you'd come see us when you were ready." His eyes shifted to Benny, lingering for a beat. "And by the looks of it...you're ready now."

She could hug her dad. In fact, that's exactly what she was going to do. Rising from her stool, she rounded the counter and launched herself at him. He let out a throaty chuckle as he wrapped her into a big bear hug.

"I love you, Dad," she mumbled into his shoulder.

"I love you too, Bethy."

She didn't even care that her mom was still icy, she'd thaw eventually. Her dad telling her everything was okay, that was all she needed to hear. What she'd been waiting for.

Eventually she pulled back, giving her dad a beaming smile before returning to her seat.

"We heard Doug left town, went back to Denver." It was her mom who spoke this time.

She'd heard that, too. Shortly after their super fun coffee at Molly's Diner. "Makes sense," she mumbled, guilt clawing its way back into her throat.

"He dropped off some things here, before he left." *He did?* "Mostly books."

This was the first she was hearing about it. It made her wonder just how much time and space her parents had planned on giving her. Stuck in her head, she didn't reply. But Benny did.

"Great. We'll take them back with us." His hand found its way back to her thigh, catching the attention of her dad.

"So..." He coughed. "I take it you two are back together?"

Both her parents were now looking at her expectantly.

Um. How do you explain to your parents that you're not labeling the sex you're having with your ex—without sounding slutty?

"Yes, sir," Benny answered before she had a chance to figure it out. "We are."

That was not the answer she was ready to give her parents.

Her mother's expression remained blank, surprise,

surprise, while her father gave one single nod of acceptance. "Okay, then. Dinner next week?"

What?

"Sounds good." Benny grinned, shooting her a wink.

Goddamnit. What happened to no labels?

CHAPTER SIXTEEN

Bethany was pissed.

They'd left her parents twenty minutes ago and she'd asked Benny to drop her back at Lucy's apartment. That clearly wasn't happening. Instead, he'd taken her back to his house. They had plans to spend the evening together. Plans he had no intention of changing.

"Benny, I swear to God, if you get out of this truck, I will lose my shit."

Her shit was long gone. And seeing as he was on a roll, he pushed the door open, fighting back a smile when he heard her growl. By the time he rounded the vehicle and opened her door, she looked damn right murderous.

"Benny," she warned as he offered his hand. "I want to go home. Take me home."

"You mean Lucy's, or back to your parents?" Yes, it was dangerous to poke the bear, but he was pissed, too.

Making no attempt to move, Bethany's arms crossed her chest. Being sure to shoot him daggers as he stood waiting.

"You really wanna do this here, in my driveway? You sure you don't want a glass of wine to throw at me while we hash this out?"

She ignored him. Eyes still flashing with fire.

"Fine." Pinching the bridge of his nose, he took a moment to pray for patience. It didn't work. "You're angry because I didn't deny our relationship."

It wasn't a question, it was a statement, one that she answered anyway. "Yes, Benny, I am. We agreed—*no labels*...and now my parents think we're together and you're all buddy buddy with my dad and making damn dinner plans. What the actual fuck?"

Patience, remember?

"Guess what, B, the reason your parents think we're together is because...*we are* together!" He was trying real frigging hard to keep his voice at an even level. It was not easy. "Whether we use some dumbass fucking label or not...nothing is going to change what we are, NeNe."

No longer satisfied with just glaring, Bethany jumped out of his truck. Taking a step until she was in his face. "Oh yeah? And what *are we*, Benny?"

He was so over pretending this wasn't real. His feelings weren't real. It all felt pretty goddamn real to him. He may not want his heart shattering all over again, but he wasn't too stupid to realize it was already too late to protect it.

"There's a reason why you ran out on your wedding day. Same way there's a reason I've spent the last ten years single." He closed what little distance there was between them and dipped his head. His face so close to hers that their noses brushed. "You're *it* for me, NeNe. Then, now, tomorrow...it's only ever been you." She inhaled shakily, moisture clinging to the corners of her glazed eyes. "And I think I'm *it* for you, too."

His throat felt raw, his chest ached and the more she searched his eyes like he was hiding something in them, the harder his heart hammered.

Benny's hand shot up as a single tear broke free, he was thumbing it away just as another soaked his skin.

"Baby," he murmured softly. Swiping away more tears than he was mentally prepared for.

He didn't know how long they stared into each other in silence. All he knew was the evening sun was beginning to dim by the time Bethany's mouth opened, but no words came, just a strangled sob caught in her throat. He watched as her eyes closed, and she drew in a stiff breath. A moment later, it wasn't the defeat in her eyes that tore the last pieces of his heart apart, it was the words that followed.

"You broke me," she whispered.

Fuck.

He was wrecked.

"I broke me, too," he confessed just as quietly, letting his nose trace hers.

"I'm scared."

"I'm fucking terrified."

Breathing each other in, Benny let his eyes close this time.

After a minute, her quiet voice skated over his skin once more. "So, what…are we just supposed to pick up where we left off?"

"I'm pretty sure that's exactly what we've been doing."

"I'm not the same person I was when I was nineteen, Benny."

His thumb traced her cheek one last time before tipping her chin up. Then his eyes opened, slowly finding hers and staying there. Letting her see everything.

"No, NeNe, you're not." His voice came out just as ragged as he felt. "You've become everything I always knew you could be…but you're still *you*. You're still *mine*. And you still own my damn heart, and you always fucking will."

As his ears pounded and his throat dried to near dehydration, she kissed him. Hard. And he finally understood that no matter how many lies he told himself or how many times he swore he was over her—he never stood a chance. Because when it came to Bethany Mayer, Benny had always been all in. A decade hadn't changed a damn thing. It had only made him love her harder.

***

"What do you think?"

Benny took another glance around at the shitty one bed

apartment. Like the shop downstairs, it needed a new lick of paint. The dated floorboards would need a polish or maybe even replaced altogether. There was also a suspicious damp spot in the corner of the popcorn ceiling above what he was assuming was supposed to be a kitchen. In reality, it was one sad looking counter and a sink.

"I think you need to stop being ridiculous and move in with me."

Okay, while it may have only been a month since Bethany had agreed to being in an actual label covered relationship with him, they weren't exactly your typical couple.

"Benny," she huffed. "You're the one being ridiculous. We can't just move in together. It's only been a few months!"

Three months. It had been three.

His head jerked back to where Bethany stood, looking stunning in a navy pinstripe dress that clung to every single curve. Her usual confident demeanor she'd arrived with was nowhere to be found though, her hands were now twisting nervously at her waist as her gaze darted around the bare space.

"It's been fifteen years, NeNe," he countered, stalking back over to her.

"Or…" Those green eyes flashed. Her shoulders visibly softening with every step he took. He liked that. "It *was* five years…*ten* years ago."

Coming to a stop in front of her, his lips tugged into a slow smile as his hand slipped into her hair. He used his hold on her to gently tip her face up to his until their gazes locked.

"*Fifteen*, baby. That's how long I've loved you."

He didn't miss Bethany's swift inhale. He hadn't used the L word, not until today. He didn't want to scare her away. But enough was enough. There was no way he was going to let her move into this place. Not when he had a house. One he very much wanted her in every night.

She was studying him. No doubt compiling a list of questions in her head. Or a damn pros and cons list.

"Move in with me," he repeated.

"I-I," her mouth slammed shut. It opened and closed once more before she finished her sentence. "The apartment comes with the lease. It's part of the deal."

He already knew the deal she'd negotiated with the town council. She didn't want to take on the shop lease just yet, not with another year left in her residency. So, she asked them to hold it for six months. In exchange, she agreed to start renting the apartment above the shop right away. It was a good faith gesture, a kind of deposit to secure the space until she was ready to begin work on it.

"That's fine. We'll start renovations on the apartment right away. When it's done, we can start storing equipment, furniture and anything you might get for the practice over the next year."

It made sense. A head start on all the work they needed to complete would save them time and money. And having an on-site place for storage was even better.

"So, I'd pay rent but not live here?"

"Yes."

"And move in with you?"

"Yes."

"Then I'd be paying rent twice? That's dumb."

What was dumb was that she still wasn't getting it.

"B, why the hell would you be paying me rent?" She went to answer, sassy narrow eyes scolding him. "You're *mine*, which makes my place yours."

Bethany snorted. "*Benny*," she chastised.

"*Bethany*," he mimicked.

"You're insane."

"And you're stubborn." Benny dipped his head until their mouths lined up. "Move in with me."

"Benny." She sighed. "I—"

"Move in with me," he said again. Cutting her off. He wasn't going to give her time to overthink. He'd thought enough about it for both of them.

Letting his lips brush hers, he repeated his demand. "Move in with me, baby." Another brush, this time his touch lingered, long enough to swipe his tongue across the seam. "Let me love you the way I want to, NeNe."

He captured her lips that were already parted and waiting. Swallowing Bethany's whimper as he used his free hand to grip her hips and haul her body into him.

This was a fight he was determined to win, and he was willing to play dirty.

CHAPTER SEVENTEEN

"You're moving in with him?" Lucy looked just as confused as Bethany felt.

"I don't know what happened." Bethany shook her head. "One minute I was showing him the apartment and the next I was agreeing to move in with him."

That was a lie. She knew exactly what happened. Benny had not only dropped the L word, he'd also worked his voodoo sex magic on her with his stupid mouth. His clever fingers. And his giant...

Okay, stop!

The point was, she'd been put in a compromising situation where she would have basically agreed to anything. And did.

"Anyway." Bethany shook her head, she was getting distracted. "Tell me more about this Mark guy?"

Lucy turned back to the vanity to continue doing her make up. Bethany had helped curl giant waves into her hair already, and was now sitting on the bathtub edge, watching her friend get ready for a date.

"Uh," Lucy pulled a tube of mascara out of her shiny pink bag and started applying it to her long lashes. "He just moved back from the city, apparently, he grew up here. Well, he went to Goldacre High, so near here, anyway. And his parents live in Woodvalley now."

"Does that mean he's living with his parents?" Bethany

frowned. "How old is he?"

Lucy shot her a 'really' look in the mirror. "People in glass houses, B!" she reprimanded. She supposed she deserved that. Who was she to judge when she was still crashing on her friend's couch. "And he's thirty."

"And you met on one of those apps?"

"Yep."

"You're seriously not gonna give me any more details?"

Bethany was trying her hardest to not make tonight's date a big deal. But it *was* a big deal. A huge fucking deal. Lucy, her shy friend, did not date. Ever. And other than admiring the odd movie stars' physique in passing while they watched a film, she never, ever, talked about guys. And when Bethany asked about her romantic life, she was shut down. Quickly.

When Lucy remained quiet, Bethany tried again. "How come you didn't tell me you were on the apps? I could've helped vet these guys for you! Which reminds me, I'm gonna need his full name and number and his parent's address. Oh, and I'm totally adding your tracking details to my phone."

No answer. It didn't deter her.

"Do I at least get to see a picture of the dude? Make sure he doesn't have crazy eyes?"

Lucy scoffed as she swapped her mascara for pressed powder and began padding her face. "You're the only one with crazy eyes right now, B."

Bethany threw her hands up in frustration. "Give me something, Luce. Come on! I've never once heard you talk about a guy, let alone go on a date. I'm dying here. Take pity on me. Tell me something. Anything." She was not above begging.

"Fine." Lucy spun around to face her. "He's got kind eyes."

"Kind eyes?" Is she freaking kidding? "Luce, you don't break a twenty-nine-year non-dating streak for *kind fricking eyes.* You break it 'cause the dude is damn close to melting your

panties off every time he's in touching distance. 'Cause you want to know what his chest will taste like when you run your tongue over it. 'Cause you can't stop thinking about his big—"

"Okay!" Lucy cried. "I get it. Stop. Please don't finish that sentence. Jeez."

"Let me see his profile." Bethany sighed, her hand outstretched, waiting patiently for Lucy to pass over her phone.

Thankfully, her friend didn't put up a fight. Probably because she was scared Bethany was going to start talking about big dicks. Which, incidentally, she was totally prepared to do.

Bethany scrolled while her brow furrowed. Dear God, this man was dull personified.

Apparently, Mark was 'just your average guy' who likes 'eating food' and 'laughing'—as if the rest of the world population didn't.

"Stop rolling your eyes!" Lucy scolded despite being back in front of the mirror, applying blush.

Bethany ignored her and continued to swipe through Mark's pictures. The man wasn't ugly, she'd give him that, but he wasn't overly attractive either. *I guess he's right about the average thing, after all.* She was still struggling to get the appeal. In her humble opinion, Lucy was way out of his league.

Maybe he has a good personality?

The lazy answers on his dating profile didn't exactly back that theory up, but not everyone is good at talking about themselves she reminded herself.

"Other than his *kind eyes*, what else caught your attention?" she prodded. "What do you guys talk about?"

She watched as Lucy shrugged at her reflection. "Nothing special, the usual. Work. What we ate. What we're watching. Things like that."

"Okay," Bethany said slowly. "But...like in a flirty way, right? Like, *wait until you taste my cherry pie* kinda thing?"

Lucy turned again, pure disgust curling her lips. "What

the hell is wrong with you?"

Bethany laughed so hard her stomach hurt. She couldn't help herself. Not because there were so many things wrong with her. Too many to count. No. She laughed because her friend looked like the idea of flirting made her want to hurl. And it made her want to tease her more. Give her some more lines she could use on her date.

"You don't like that one?" she asked between giggles. "Okay, okay. How about...*you wanna frost my cupcake, Big Boy?*"

"You're sick!" Lucy stomped, fighting a smile Bethany totally spotted before storming back into her bedroom.

She was up and chasing her a second later. "Too much? Okay. What about...*Is that a baguette in your pocket or are*—"

"Don't finish that sentence!" Lucy snapped. The twinkle in her eyes betraying the scowl she was giving her. "If I let you track me, will you promise to stop talking?"

Bethany bit her lip. Preventing her from blurting out the glazed donut joke she'd just thought of. *Safety first.* She did want to track her. She'd watched enough documentaries to know most serial killers were average white guys. Like Mark. Some of them even lived with their parents.

Oh God, please tell me he doesn't live in the basement?

***

The next day, Bethany woke up feeling off. Restless. She couldn't quite put her finger on what was bothering her, she just had this weird twinge in her stomach that kept making itself known. It's how she found herself at Molly's, despite there being a pile of notes and textbooks back at the apartment that she was supposed to be buried under. She needed a distraction. Her best friend. And quite possibly a milkshake.

"Don't you have better things to do?" Lucy frowned as she continued to wipe down the counter.

"Nope." Bethany gave her a toothy grin.

It was obviously a lie. One she hoped her friend wasn't going to call her on. Even if she didn't feel like studying, she should probably be packing. Benny might be busy at work today, but they still planned on moving her things into his place this weekend. Yes, she only had three measly suitcases, but they weren't going to pack themselves. "You never told me how your date went?" she smoothly changed the subject.

Judging by her friend's grimace she was taking it that Mark wasn't going to be getting a second date.

Lucy sighed, blowing out an extra-long breath. "Apparently he was close to making it big as a professional juggler."

"What?" Bethany almost choked on air. "A professional juggler?"

Lucy rolled her eyes as she braced her hands on the steel surface. "Yep. Even decided to give me a little demonstration of his *skills*."

Just from the way Lucy elongated the word "skills", Bethany had a pretty good idea of where this conversation was heading, and she couldn't help but smile.

"What even constitutes a professional juggler," she air quoted the word for emphasis. "The circus?"

Her bestie scoffed. "He wishes."

She stifled a giggle and pasted on her most serious expression. "Poor Mark. You don't believe he's got what it takes?"

"He gave me a demonstration." Lucy's brow lifted as she fought like a trooper to suppress her grin.

"And? I'm on the edge of my seat here, Luce."

"Well, let's just say there were only two balls, and he kept dropping them both. Did I also happen to mention that this demonstration went on for *an hour*. In a public place. With witnesses."

Oh dear. Her poor, poor friend.

Just as she was about to give in to temptation and let her laugh break free, her phone went off. Which was odd enough to have her answering. No one actually rang her anymore. She was more of a 'I'll text you back five hours later' kind of girl.

"Hello?" she swiped, not recognizing the caller ID.

"Bethany?" A panicked female voice asked. "Uh, it's Libby. Zach's wife."

Libby? Why was Libby calling her?

"Hey, what's up?" She sat up a bit straighter, more than aware of the frantic energy crackling down the phone line. And there was that sinking feeling again.

"It's, uh, have you seen the news?" Bethany's stomach twisted. "The guys, they've been fighting a wildfire over by Splitrock all day." Another twist. Libby's voice was quiet for a second before she tore her world apart. "Zach and Benny...they're still out there."

Bethany stopped listening after that. But she kept her phone to her ear as she slipped off the diner stool and started heading for the exit. Ignoring her best friend's calls from behind her.

"I'm on my way over there now," Bethany announced, pushing open the glass door.

"I'm coming, too." Libby's voice trembled. "I'll meet you there."

***

The place was carnage.

The scent of burnt earth filling Bethany's throat as her grip on Libby's hand tightened. Ever since they'd arrived, they'd been clinging onto each other. Both desperate to hear good news. It was Cody who had led them to where they both stood next to his cruiser. Away from the red tape cordoning off the hot zone.

Their eyes remained fixed on the fire line. Looking for something. Anything. They'd still not seen the other men on Benny's team. Bethany hoped like hell that was a good thing. That they were out there, looking for them. Cody had disappeared not long after they arrived. He said he'd gone in search of answers, but the worry on his face made her think he just couldn't handle the total fear and devastation vibrating off the two of them.

He's going to be okay. This is his job. He's trained for this exact situation.

She clung desperately to those thoughts. Repeating them over and over again in her head.

All they knew, all they'd been told was that during the battle to put out the fire, the wind shifted before Benny and Zach had a chance to retreat with the rest of the team, which meant they couldn't escape the way they came. They had to find another way. When she'd gone to Google what that meant, Cody had taken her phone. Literally taken it. Like she was a child. He was lucky she was using all her current strength to keep breathing or his balls and her knee would be getting acquainted.

It's for the best. Google will scare the shit out of you.

It would. And she was already scared shitless.

"I'm pregnant." Libby choked on a sob. "I took your advice, and I guess it worked 'cause I'm finally pregnant. We found out today."

No. No. No.

Fuck.

Twisting to face Libby, Bethany's hand went to the woman's shoulders. Holding her in place as her body vibrated with more sobs.

"Listen to me, Libby. They're okay. They're going to be okay. The guys are gonna get them. We have to trust them. They're good at what they do. Okay?"

She didn't feel nearly as strong as the words she spoke, but that didn't matter. Libby needed her to be strong. And so did Benny.

They both nodded at each other, a silent understanding to try their hardest not to think the worst. Not yet.

"They're going to be okay," Libby repeated Bethany's words.

Please God, let them be okay.

CHAPTER EIGHTEEN

This was bad. Really fucking bad.

They were supposed to be out. But the wind turned. Now Benny and Zach were stuck with nothing but static coming from their radios and flames filling the sky.

"We need to move. Find a black zone." Zach's gaze went to the dry brush surrounding them. "We've got maybe a minute."

Benny was already grabbing the fire shelters from his pack and shoving one in Zach's hand. "Over there." He pointed behind his friend. "There's bare ground over that rise."

One nod and they were running. Low and fast and trying not to cough through the masks that didn't feel like they were doing what they were supposed to be doing anymore.

Flames were still leaping behind them. Smoke thinning the air and pressing down on his chest as he dropped to his knees and ripped open the aluminum foil blanket.

His heart was pounding. His mind racing. They could do this. This is what they were trained for.

Zach's voice cracked through the smoke as he spoke again. "We can't fucking die. *I* can't fucking die. Libby's pregnant."

Jesus fucking Christ.

His mind went to Bethany. *His* woman. Would the guys call her? What if they didn't? What if they did? Was she out there now, waiting for him? Was she scared…upset?

No. Focus.

But his thoughts were on Bethany. How could they not be? The look on her face when she'd spotted him on the highway flashed before him. Her whispered words that became his undoing, *I'm yours.* The thought of her scared. Worried. It was too much. Too painful to think about.

Then get your head in the game. Make sure you stay alive.

"We're not gonna fucking die," he shouted back, willing himself to believe it.

Placing his boots on the edge, his face went down, his feet facing the flames.

Zach did the same before shouting, "Seal it tight and don't move."

The heat was immediate as he curled inside, sealing the edges with his gloved hands. He tried his best to breathe through it. The dry oven like heat. The flames licking the foil. The earth vibrating beneath him. It was the longest twenty minutes of his life. He spent them thinking of Bethany. Her beautiful face. Her husky laugh that made his whole body warm. The addictive scent of her rose scented bodywash that lingered on his bedsheets long after she left. His woman. The love of his life. A life that had only just started.

Benny's eyes were getting heavy. It didn't take a genius to figure out he was severely dehydrated now, and he'd inhaled way too much smoke. But he needed to stay awake. He needed to fucking survive. For her. For Zach. For Libby.

The faint sounds of boots crunching and muffled voices was the only thing that kept him from collapsing.

Just hold on a bit longer.

He could do that. He would do that. Zach could, too.

Please God, let Zach be okay.

He felt the shelter peel back, his eyes trying their best to readjust as more smoke hit his lungs. Forcing a cough from him that was hard enough to cause him to hit the ground.

"Fuck. You scared the shit out of us."

Luke's gruff voice was the last thing he heard before everything went black.

CHAPTER NINETEEN

It had been nineteen hours. Benny had been unconscious for nineteen goddamn hours. And the hospital staff were just carrying on as if that was normal. News flash—it's not normal.

Zach, who was sheltered side by side with Benny when they found them, was fine. Freaking dandy. He hadn't passed out. And with a couple of fluid IVs, he'd been discharged. It wasn't that Bethany wasn't relieved that Zach was okay, she was, she was just so damn worried about her man.

My man?

Damnit. He *was* her man, and she'd never told him. Not when there wasn't an orgasm on the line, anyway. The whole time, they'd been doing what they'd been doing, he had been the one to show his cards. Declare his love. Tell her she was *it* for him. And what had she done? Nodded along. She may have agreed to the direction he was taking things, but she'd never given him the words. The truth.

I need to tell him.

That was going to be really fricking hard considering he was still unconscious.

You need to wake up, Benny. Please, wake up. I love you. So much it hurts.

Swatting the tears before they fell, she straightened. She needed to keep it together. No falling apart until she got more information.

She'd been hovering outside the glass door of Benny's room in the ICU for a few minutes. Her eyes scanning the main floor. So over being told he was 'stable', she was determined to get more answers. Results. Anything that would help her piece this puzzle together. Ideally, before Benny's mom and dad returned from their coffee run.

Gotcha.

The ICU attending finally made an appearance. Wasting no time, she was striding toward the silver-haired middle-aged man a moment later. She almost felt guilty as she reached for his arm just before he could get to the staff room door, he looked tired.

Yeah. Well. I'm tired, too.

"Dr. Win? I hope you don't mind...but I just had a couple more questions about Benjamin Tucker...the firefighter in room twelve," she choked out. Trying her hardest not to sound as desperate as she felt.

The man's crinkled eyes gentled as he turned to her. Giving a calm yet assertive nod before encouraging her to continue.

"His EEG?"

An EEG was a test that measures electrical activity in the brain, a test they'd done on Benny earlier to check for seizure activity and to help evaluate his brain function. No one had updated them on the outcome, so she was assuming everything was okay. No news is good news and all that. But knowledge was power.

Because knowledge is going to go real well with your current crippling anxiety?

Now really wasn't the time to troll herself.

Shut up and listen to the doctor!

"We've got neuro monitoring. No seizure activity. But...brain functions are sluggish. We're giving it time. Sedation was minimal."

Damn.

"The CT?"

"Clean. No swelling, no bleeding. No obvious hypoxic injury."

That was good at least, although it didn't sound like they were out of the woods yet.

"Why isn't he waking up?" Her voice was thick, her tears threatening to spill again any minute.

Dr. Win's sympathetic brown eyes held her in place. "His body went through hell. It needs time. *He* needs time."

"How much more time?" Nineteen freaking hours seemed like a lot of time to her.

"Ms. Mayer, right?" She nodded, resisting the urge to make him call her doctor. Mostly because she didn't feel like one right now. She felt like the overly emotional girlfriend she was. "Your boyfriend is a fighter. He's doing better than most would. Just trust him. Trust us."

She nodded again. Trying her best to hold it together. Just for a bit longer.

When Bethany returned to Benny's room, she didn't find his parents inside like she expected. Instead, sitting next to his bedside was Luke.

"Hey," she greeted, taking a seat on the opposite side of the bed.

Luke looked rough. Like he hadn't slept, either. "Hey, sweetheart." He gave her a weak smile. "The guys wanted to come see him, you don't mind us taking turns coming in, do you?"

She shook her head. She knew Benny's teammates filled the waiting room. Even Zach and Libby remained after getting the all clear. She was both surprised and grateful they hadn't insisted on visiting his room until now. ICU had strict visitor rules, and they'd already pushed the two person at a time limit with Bethany and both of Benny's parents being in his room for the past nineteen hours.

Both their gazes went to the hospital wires hooked up to Benny. You'd think after staring at them for so long, she'd be used to the sight. She wasn't. Just like every other time her eyes lingered for too long, they began to mist.

"He's too damn stubborn to die, B. Knowing Benny, he'd drag himself back just to tell me I'm full of shit." Luke's gruff voice had her glancing back up and the beginnings of a smile forming. "I wouldn't put it past the fucker to be waiting for the right moment to open his eyes—like when he decides I've been talking to his girl a little too long."

That sounded exactly like something Benny would do. The thought alone enough to ease some of the tightness in her chest as she whispered a "thank you" to Luke.

His chin dipped at her thanks. Then he stood, clearing his throat and muttering, "Hunter's up next," before heading for the door.

Bethany laced her fingers with Benny's. She needed to touch him while she internally screamed at him to wake up. She couldn't lose him. Not again. She barely survived the first time and everyone was still breathing. Her heart had only just found its way back to him, how was it supposed to keep beating without him?

A strangled sob made her body vibrate. She let the tears fall. She'd give herself one minute to fall apart. One minute to let the fear take over. Then she'd dry her eyes and get her shit together.

Thirty more seconds.

She shook harder. A whimper escaping as her head dropped to her lap.

"D-don't c-cry."

Bethany stopped breathing. Her gaze flying up in disbelief until she was looking into Benny's bloodshot eyes. She still couldn't breathe. But she forced herself to blink. Worried this wasn't real.

Pinch yourself, too!

"B-baby. Please." His voice cracked again. Each word sounded like it was being forcibly dragged from his throat.

It was real. Benny was awake. And just like that, she could finally breathe.

***

"B, baby?" Bethany ignored Benny and continued to load up his bedside table with water and snacks. "NeNe?" he tried again. And when that didn't work, he whined, "Bethany?"

She was not doing this. Not again.

"No, Benny." She attempted to scold him, but the mock-stern expression she was going for only made him smile wider.

Benny had only just been discharged and after resisting the urge to shower with him, she was tucking him into bed. Like a good girlfriend.

"It's *technically* a form of self-care," he argued. "No? Okay. It's good for morale?"

She fought back her own smile and decided on a dramatic huff instead. "Yeah, yeah," she scoffed. "You know what else is good for morale? Being able to breathe. So how about, you stop flashing that chest at me until we get the all clear on your inflamed lungs next week, okay?"

This was hard for her, too. She'd almost lost him. Again. Which meant all she wanted to do was climb him like a tree and never let go.

Benny's head dipped to his bare chest, his gaze coming back to her complete with a devilishly sexy smirk.

"You like what you see, baby?" He winked.

"You're a doofus."

"Want me to get up, give you a little show…maybe turn around and show you the back? I *may* or *may not* have forgotten to put boxer shorts on."

A giggle broke free just as he whipped up the sheet his lap had been covered with.

"Oh my God, Benjamin Tucker, you put that thing away before you take my eye out," she snorted.

"Is *that* why you're keeping both eyes on it, NeNe?"

"Funny," she deadpanned, but instead of leaving him to rest, like she should, she crawled into bed next to him.

She wanted to hold him. Pinch herself again, maybe him

147

too, just to check. He was here. Alive. And all hers.

"I want a cuddle," she demanded as her head went to his chest.

Benny slipped back down the headboard, taking them both with him. Readjusting until they were lying flat and his arm held her tight.

"I'm okay," he reassured her for the millionth time. "I'm sorry I scared you."

"I don't need your apology; I just need you to promise me that you'll never die. Or you won't die until you're like a hundred or something, and only after I've died. Okay? Promise?"

Benny's husky chuckle was quiet, but his body still shook. "Is that all?"

"Benny."

"Okay, baby. I promise. No dying until I'm a hundred."

Burying further into his chest, she let her fingers brush the dusting of dark hair over muscle.

They fell into a comfortable quiet. Benny's hold loosening just enough to trail his fingers up and down the side of her crop top. Lingering longer on the exposed flesh that was now covered in goosebumps.

"I thought I was going to lose you again," Bethany admitted to Benny's pectoral muscles while the man himself dotted soft kisses into her hair. "I don't think I'd survive it."

Way to make someone else's near death experience about yourself, Bethany.

She really wished her head would shut the fuck up. She was having a moment. It needed to chill.

Where's your chill?

"I'm not going anywhere, NeNe. You're stuck with me."

"You promise?"

More kisses covered the top of her head. "I promise."

"I love you, Benny." She felt him suck in a breath but hurried on before she lost her nerve. "I don't think I ever stopped loving you. And the more I think about it, the more I realize that you were right...that's why I couldn't marry

Doug." The tears she thought she'd left at the hospital were back with a vengeance, but she was going to power through. "Because my heart belonged to someone else. It belonged to you. I gave it to you willingly at fourteen and you never gave it back."

Benny rolled them over until she was on her back looking up at his darkening eyes. "Are you kidding me right now?"

"What?" She sniffed. Surely, he couldn't be mad at her for declaring her love?

"You can't tell me you love me. Tell me I own your heart. Make me feel like the air's been punched out of me. And then expect me not to take you. Show you just how much I fucking love you, too. And how my heart has only ever and will always be yours."

Goddamnit. She wanted that, too. She was beginning to wish she'd waited a bit longer to declare her love.

Nope. You waited too frigging long as it is.

To stop herself rubbing against him like a cat in heat, she decided to lighten the mood. A smile tugging at her lips as she widened her eyes with feigned innocence. "Oops."

"Oops. Seriously?" That mischievous smile was back. "You've got one week, baby. Then this ass is getting reddened."

"Don't threaten me with a good time, Benjamin Tucker."

Then he kissed her. And just like that, everything in the world felt right again.

CHAPTER TWENTY

"What's that?"

Bethany was pointing at the last of her things that Benny had asked Lucy to bring over. It had been over a week since he'd been discharged and despite spending every day and night with him, she'd still not officially moved in. Which is why he'd taken matters into his own hands and done it for her.

"Your last suitcase and a box of books from your parent's place," he stated the obvious. "Welcome home, B. Time to start unpacking don't you think?"

She may have her stuff in their house, but she'd not filled the closet space he'd made for her. Her toiletries were in a neat pile instead of in their vanity. And her laptop was neatly tucked away in its case every night instead of being left on the table. Like he'd told her to do.

He was sick of it. He wanted her things everywhere. For her to make this place a home. Her home. Forever.

She was chewing her lip again. Looking unsure.

"Baby." He went to her frozen form in the middle of the living room and turned her to face him while his hands went to her shoulders. "It's time. This place is yours now, too. I want you to put your stamp on it. Decorate it however you like. Order a bunch of clown paintings for all I care. Go crazy. Just please, for the love of God, unpack your things. It's driving me insane seeing you live out of suitcases."

"Clown paintings?" She lifted a brow before hitting him with that dazzling smile. "Well…" Her pointer finger tapped those plump pink lips as humor danced in those deep jade eyes. "I did see this toilet paper holder I liked the other day…it plays Eye of the Tiger."

"That's terrifying." He bit back the laugh bubbling in his chest.

"Or…*motivational*," she corrected. Goddamn he loved this woman.

"Have I told you how much I love you today?" Lowering his head until their faces were just inches apart, he breathed in her familiar rose scent.

"You love me?" she teased, purposefully widening her eyes.

"Want me to prove it?"

Please say yes.

He'd been given the all clear yesterday for light activity. Not that there was anything light about what he wanted to do to her.

"And how exactly do you plan on proving it?" Dainty hands settled on his waist as she let her chest bump into his. He fought back a groan. She was so fucking soft. Made just for him.

Inching closer, he let his lips ghost the shell of her ear, reveling in her shiver as his breath sunk into her skin. "That depends on you, baby. You want a list…or a demonstration?"

Bethany pressed herself against him, giving a slow twist of her hips and being sure to graze a part of him that was only getting harder by the second.

Then her mouth was doing the taunting as she brushed it over his, her tongue darting out to lick her lower lip before whispering into him.

"I think I'm gonna need you to show me."

That was all he needed to hear. Benny's hands slid down until they were on her ass. With a quick bend of the knees, she was airborne a second later, her legs wrapping around his waist as he carried her into the kitchen. He needed a solid surface.

As soon as he'd deposited her on the island, his mouth came crashing down onto hers. His fingers getting lost in thick brown waves as he angled her head to get deeper.

She tasted like caramel-kissed coffee with a hint of rose. Sweet, warm and all fucking his. More whimpers slid down his throat as his free hand went to the buttons on her jean shorts. Next thing he knew, her hands were there, too. Tugging the zipper and helping him drag the denim down her long-tanned legs.

With every swipe, more sugar coated his tongue. And with every moan, the pounding in his ears grew louder. She was addictive.

Using his thumb, Benny guided her panties to one side, giving him room to drag two of his fingers down her center until it was his turn to groan.

My girl is always so ready for me.

She was also ready to swallow down his groans as she took the kiss deeper, circling her hands around his shoulders and holding him close.

He pushed one finger inside her, then another, kissing her that much harder as she gasped for air. She felt like heaven. He kept still, the hand that was no longer in her hair, going to her hip to keep her in place.

She was squirming when he released her lips, just the way he liked it. He waited patiently until heavy-lidded eyes met his.

"You're gonna watch." His gaze dipped to where they joined, hers followed.

With her eyes fixed on his hand, he began to move. Slowly gliding in and out while his thumb pressed into that sweet spot.

"Oh, God." Bethany flung her head back.

"Eyes on us, NeNe." His warning sounded just as feral as he felt. "You're gonna watch yourself come undone. First on my fingers. Then on my dick. And then I'm gonna hold you down and make you fall apart on my mouth again and again—until you're ruined, baby. Just the way you like it."

"Fuck," she breathed, her body thrashing as she struggled to keep her gaze down.

"Can you take another finger?"

His lips began to tilt as he watched her nod frantically, labored breaths and the satisfying sounds of how turned on his woman was filling the air.

Easing another finger inside, he growled as he felt her grip him.

The sight of Bethany on their kitchen island, legs wide open for him, watching and taking everything he gave her, was the sexiest goddamn thing he'd ever seen.

"That's it, B. You're always gonna take what I give you, aren't you?" She whimpered in reply, her hips desperately trying to match his movements thrust for thrust.

She was close. So damn close.

"This is *mine. All fucking mine.* Say it."

"It's yours." She gasped. "It's all yours."

Increasing pressure on that little bundle of nerves, he curled his fingers inside her.

"Let me see you make a mess, baby. Show your man what he does to you."

He could feel her tightening around him and he couldn't take anymore. He needed to taste her again. Slamming his mouth onto her, he muffled her moans as she trembled against him. Kissing her through every shake and every sigh until she was boneless in his arms.

"You're gonna marry me, Bethany Mayer." He was still panting as he pulled back.

Her eyes flew open, love and lust colliding as she answered.

"Yes, Benjamin Tucker. I'm gonna marry you."

Damn fucking right she was.

EPILOGUE

Six months later

Benny and Bethany stood in the old tool shop hand in hand. Their gazes sweeping the empty space.

He was so proud of her. This was all hers. Her very own practice. She was going to change the lives of everyone in their town.

You're engaged to a doctor, dude!

He still couldn't believe it. Not that Bethany had come back. And certainly not that he'd convinced her to marry him. All it had taken was him sliding a ring onto her finger while she slept and a rather cheeky argument that *technically* she'd already agreed to marry him. The fact that she didn't put up a fight said it all. He was one lucky son-of-a-bitch.

Bethany squeezed his hand in excitement. "Where do we start?"

We.

He'll never get sick of hearing that. They were a, *we*. A team. Partners. Soulmates.

Sappy much?

His inner voice could go to hell. He'd waited what felt like a lifetime for Bethany, he'd earned the right to be a sappy bastard.

"Wherever you want." They may be a *we*, but this was all hers, she called the shots. He was just along for the ride.

"You tell me what you want and in what order and I'll find a way to make it happen."

"How did I get so lucky?" she asked as she leaned into him.

"You *are* damn lucky. I'm a catch," he teased, tugging her hand and pulling her further into the room. He dodged her swat and grinned like a fool. "Easy, NeNe, you don't want to piss off the help, do you?"

"You're lucky you're pretty." She narrowed her eyes on him but didn't bother to hide her smile.

"No...*you're* lucky I'm pretty." This time he wasn't quick enough to dodge the whack to his stomach.

"Okay, okay. Enough violence. Let's check out the other rooms before the guys get here."

They needed some sort of plan before they started delegating jobs. Benny had a few ideas, but it all depended on what they were starting with.

"Who's coming?" Bethany's hand fell away as she moved toward the back room.

"Well, Cody is obviously busy." Cat gave birth to a healthy baby boy three months ago. "And Zach and Libby have an appointment up in Goldacre." Libby was going on seven months pregnant, so Zach was unlikely to be able to help much over the coming months. "But the rest of the Evans brothers have volunteered to help—so Wade, Matt and Jonah will be here. Then, of course, Luke and Hunter."

Bethany nodded to herself as her fingers ran over the dilapidated walls. It reminded him of the walls upstairs. They didn't look like that anymore, though. Not after months of blood, sweat and tears. He was suddenly grateful they'd finished doing up the apartment before they made a start on this project. It meant it was one less thing to worry about.

"I think we should make it a blank slate. Floors first. Then the walls. Then we can add counters, shelves, cupboards after."

"And the back room?"

"That, we'll have to contract out—I want a kitchen, and bathrooms put in, that's beyond our skill set."

Fair enough. He would speak to Wade about contractors, not long ago he'd converted a barn on their ranch into a restaurant, so he was most likely to have the contacts they needed.

"It's gonna look great, baby." His gaze darted around the space once more. He could already picture it.

"You know the best part?" Bethany asked, swaying those sexy hips his way.

"What's that?"

"That the fire station is just next door." Oh, he hadn't forgotten. "Maybe we can have sneaky rendezvouses?"

They were absolutely going to have sneaky rendezvouses.

"Damn straight." He pulled her into him, not waiting for their bodies to even meet before his mouth was on her.

Yep. One lucky son-of-a-bitch.

***

Two weeks later

You wouldn't think that the thick low gray clouds were out in force today. Or that most of the Woodvalley fields lay under a blanket of ice. Not while Bethany was in the warm and inviting home of Cat and Cody, complete with a huge fire blazing next to overly stuffed leather couches and large oak tables filled with all the essential January comfort foods.

Speaking of which, she slyly filled her plate with her third helping of chili and fluffy buttermilk biscuits.

Don't mind if I do.

Today was a small gathering, just the guys from the fire station and their respective partners. Oh, and Lucy, who Bethany dragged everywhere. Cat and Cody's latest addition to their family, baby Lucas, was ready to be shown off. And while they'd all visited and met Lucas individually, this was his first time being around so many of them all at once.

Bethany's gaze went to Dylan, Cody and Cat's eldest at eleven-years-old. He seemed so much more grown up since she first met him last summer. She could tell just by the way he was holding Lucas, with so much care, that he was going to be an amazing big brother.

"I want one," Benny whispered into her ear as he slid up beside her. Holding his own plate of chili and biscuits.

"You want one, what?" She tilted her head in question.

"A baby. I want one."

Good thing her mouth wasn't full, or chili would be all over the colorful shaggy rug they were standing on.

"Um." She coughed. *Am I choking on air?* "Y-you want a baby?"

A sexy smirk graced his lips. "Don't worry, I'm not talking tomorrow. My woman has got important shit she needs to do first. But in a few years, yeah, I want one. I want a mini-Bethany running around pulling my hair and calling me a doofus. Is that something you think you'd want?"

"A mini-me calling you a doofus?" She wasn't choking anymore. She was smiling. That image alone, as dumb as it was, it did something weird to her insides. "I mean, yeah, I could want that."

"You could want what?" Lucy asked as she joined their little huddle by the fire.

Not ready to talk babies with her bestie, she changed the subject. "Oh nothing. You try those cornbread muffins, yet? I swear I wanna bathe in that honey butter."

"Eww." Lucy grimaced while Benny laughed.

Benny was the one to change the subject next, asking Lucy about Daisy-Mae. He had a soft spot for the ginger terror. She let them talk, her eyes roaming the room as she admired her newfound family. She'd hit the jackpot not just with her fiancé but with his friends, too. All the women had been warm and welcoming to both her and Lucy. And all the men were like the brothers she never had. She was excited to do life with these people. Her attention went to the diamond on her finger, just a few more months and she'd be Doctor Bethany Tucker. She couldn't freaking wait.

"What are you doing here?" Cat may not have been in the room, but she was loud enough for everyone in it to hear her.

All eyes turned to the living room door, expectantly. Someone was clearly about to gatecrash their intimate gathering.

Cat reentered the room first, rolling her eyes and giving Cody a look that Bethany didn't recognize. Secret couple language she assumed. A moment later, a man followed behind. And she had no doubt who she was looking at. With the same midnight black hair as his sister, and striking blue-green eyes, she knew it was Jack. He was taller than she expected and had some bulk on him. Enough to stretch the crisp white shirt he had on and fill out the smart black trousers he wore. But the biggest giveaway was probably that Lucy had stopped breathing. A fact she felt the need to confirm as she let her gaze drift to her friend beside her.

Oh yeah, this is Jack, alright.

When Lucas arrived three months ago and Jack hadn't, Bethany heard through the grapevine, aka Rachel, that he'd had to stay in London for work. Cat was rightly sad. Cody pissed. But clearly, he'd managed to swindle some time off if he was here now.

"Afternoon all." With the good looks gene both Cat and Jack had been blessed with, a sexy deep voice and a goddamn British accent, she realized any woman would be in trouble around this guy. But as Jack's eyes and confident smile swept the room and landed on Lucy, she knew without question it wasn't just any woman in trouble. It was her best friend. Because that smile didn't move on. It stayed. And with every second, it grew wider.

Oh, this is gonna be fun.

SNEAK PEEK AT BOOK SEVEN IN THE LOVE BURNS SERIES

Burnout

For the first time in her life, Lucy finally understood the appeal of cursing. How else can you really do justice to her situation without releasing a string of F-bombs?

She'd take a side of *F-me* to accompany the bubbling anxiety making her chest tight. And a big old helping of *Holy-S* to describe the sweat trying to make itself known under her bra.

"You okay?" Bethany's hand went to her forearm. "I don't think you've spoken or taken a breath in the past six minutes. I'm beginning to get concerned that the lack of oxygen has cut off the supply to your brain."

Her best friend was hilarious.

"I just remembered that I forgot to leave food out for Daisy-Mae. I need to go."

Yes, she was being dramatic, and no, her cat did not need to be fed, but she didn't care. She lived a relatively drama-free life, so she was allowing herself one tiny little freak out.

"Oh no, you don't," Bethany narrowed those big green eyes on her. "I'm not letting you run just 'cause the mysterious *Jack* has arrived."

Jack Jones, the hottest man she'd ever seen in real life, had indeed just entered the room. With floppy dark hair, piercing blue green eyes, and a ridiculously symmetrical face, he was darn right dangerous. Throw in height, muscles and a designer suit and he was practically a health hazard.

The sight of him alone was clearly enough to break her. But the sight of him currently being introduced to his three-month-old nephew? She wasn't sure she'd ever recover.

Annnnnd…my ovaries just exploded.

Cool, cool.

Who was she kidding? There was nothing remotely cool about her. Which was exactly why she needed to get out of there. Before she melted into a puddle, in her friend's living room, on her pretty abstract rug.

That wouldn't be a good look.

It wouldn't be. Yet, she wouldn't put it past her traitorous body. Apparently, it had control issues around this man. Which was stupid because she'd only met him once for Pete's sake. Three years ago. When he'd shamelessly flirted with her at the diner where she worked.

Oh no. He's coming over.

Abort! Abort! Get out of there now!

Only she couldn't. Her so-called friend had noticed Jack's slow motion swagger toward her and amid Lucy's internal panic, she'd sneakily grabbed hold of her arm and was keeping it hostage.

"I hate you." She whispered to Bethany, her voice full of the venom she deserved.

"You love me." She had the audacity to laugh.

The closer he got, the hotter she felt. It may be January. And Woodvalley Pines may be under a blanket of ice outside, but under her off the shoulder cream sweater, there were some questionable things happening. She may even be forced to throw out her bra.

I love my bra.

Wow. That was a sucky thought. Great. Now she was angry, flustered *and* sad.

Just in time for Jack to enter her space. Meeting her eyes with such a fierce intensity, she felt the urge to find the nearest blanket and crawl under it.

"It's Lucy, isn't it?" His voice was deep and smoother than silk. Did she mention he had a British accent too? Because...*of course he did.* "We met a few years ago...at the diner."

He remembers me.

Unable to muster words, she nodded and tried for a smile instead.

Her failure to respond didn't seem to deter him. He took a step closer. Not caring in the slightest that his proximity was breaking every respectable social boundary.

Dear Lord, he even smelt good. Fresh, clean, and was that vanilla?

Put your tongue back in your head.

"It's okay if you don't remember me." That devilish lopsided smile went straight to her core, flipping switches she had no idea were down there. "How about I remember for the both of us?"

Oh God, he was flirting again. Here. In his sister's house. At her new baby's party. In front of everyone. Everyone who was now looking their way.

Yep. This bra is going in the trash.

Was it her or did the room just fall quiet?

"I remember." She rushed out, noticing his green gaze flash with something she didn't recognize. Something she didn't know if she wanted to recognize.

Her cheeks heated. Making her wonder if she'd gone red.

Despite the new and slightly terrifying feeling of burning from the inside out, she couldn't look away. Not when he dragged his tongue slowly across his lower teeth and not when he let his gaze fall. Trailing down the curve of her sweater, skimming the fit of her jeans, and lingering on her scuffed brown ankle boots. Then, just as slowly, his eyes slid back up, inch by inch, like he was tracing the fire he'd lit under her skin.

"That's good." It may have just been her imagination, but she could have sworn his voice just dropped. "That's *really good.*"

DON'T MISS THE REST OF THE BOOKS IN THE LOVE BURNS SERIES

Toasted

Welcome to Woodvalley Pines...where hunky firefighters save the day! It's time to turn up the heat and hope this smokin' hot fireman can control the blaze.

Libby hadn't even been in Woodvalley Pines a day and she was already freaking out. Her kitchen had just set on fire. From toast of all things! That's right, she was the victim of the elusive toaster fire. Yes, a toaster. Who knew they could just spontaneously burst into flames? She certainly didn't. If that wasn't enough to ruin her day, a swarm of hot firefighters seeing her in her pink pajamas would do it.

Zach tried his hardest not to laugh as the woman in the Disney pajamas accused him of keeping toaster fire safety a secret. He didn't know where in the world this angry green-eyed princess had come from, but he had to admit that he was intrigued. After all, if she had this much passion when it came to talking toasters, what other kind of flames could he stoke in her?

Libby and Zach's spark was instant, but will the fire burn out or can they keep the flames blazing?

Isobel Reed's snarky humorous romances have fans fanning themselves as they devour the stories. Her books are one-clicks for readers who love Lori Wilde's - The First Love Cookie Club and Jennifer Ryan's - At Wolf Ranch books. Readers will struggle not to fall for the sexy small town heroes and the sassy women who claim them!

EXCERPT:

"You okay, ma'am? Neighbor reported he heard screaming."

Oh shit.

"Oh, yeah. There was screaming. I mean, yes, I did scream. But it was more like a release, y'know? Like, when you're having a really shitty day and you scream into a pillow. It was kinda like that." *For the love of God, stop talking.* "Anyway, yeah, I'm fine. All good. Hunky-dory."

Hunky-dory? Really? And screaming into pillows? Way to embarrass yourself in front of the handsome firefighters. Are your Disney pajamas not enough humiliation for you? Do you want to detail your hair removal regime next?

Luckily, the other man decided not to comment. He simply nodded, for which Libby was grateful. Once he'd given Zach a quick update on the cause of the fire – that blasted toaster – he disappeared and left the two of them alone again.

Turns out, just the mention of the toaster was enough to bring back her rage.

"Did you know toasters just sometimes set on fire? When exactly did that become a thing? And why aren't there more people talking about it?"

Zach incorrectly thought that clearing his throat would be enough to mask his snigger. "Uh, well, any old appliances can be a potential fire hazard. With toasters, a build-up of breadcrumbs can also act as fuel to the fire."

"What the hell? I didn't know that, Zach. Why didn't I know that? Is this some big firefighter secret or something? 'Cause I'm telling you right now, people need to know this! I'm thirty-one, Zach. *Thirty-one!* And never in my life would I have thought I could be making toast one day and then … *boom!* Fire! People need to be told. They need to know, damnit!"

Okay, it was safe to say this was not her finest moment. She was well aware ranting about toaster fires while sitting on the curb – in just her miniscule, bright pink shorts and vest top – was giving off batshit crazy vibes. But she clearly just couldn't help herself. Once she got a look at his expression, the crazy continued.

"Are you laughing at me?"

"No, ma'am."

"You are … you're laughing at me!"

"Smiling. I'm smiling at you. There's a big difference."

Cop-Off

Return to Woodvalley Pines...where a sexy police officer comes across one troublemaker that he's determined to pin down.

Cat is looking to snag herself a cowboy. After all, what else is there to do in the small town of Woodvalley Pines. And after the year she's had, she deserves to treat herself. There's only one problem. Cody freaking McBride. The devil himself. And the bane of her existence. It's bad enough she has to look at his smug face most days, but now he's made it his mission to meddle in her love life. Which means only one thing, it's about to get ugly.

Single dad and local cop Cody thought he was done with love. He was content in his routine. Work, eat, sleep, repeat. But then Cat shows up in town. Lighting fires wherever she goes and hurling insults his way while she's doing it. He actually finds himself enjoying fighting with the little she-devil, it's the most alive he's felt in years.

Woodvalley Pines is about to witness the ultimate showdown. Where clothes aren't the only things getting torn to shreds.

Cop-Off is set in a small town filled with sassy heroines, hunky heroes, and busybodies who can't help but share their two cents. Fans of Any Man of Mine by Rachel Gibson and Worth the Risk by Jamie Beck will love Isobel Reed's steamy, snarky romance!

EXCERPT:

"You cannot write that!" Libby gasped, handing Cat back her phone.

"Why not?"

"Because you're going to attract the wrong kind of man!"

Why her friend seemed so horrified, Cat had no idea. All she'd done was show her the profile she'd set up on a local dating app. It had been Libby's idea to get back out there in the first place. That was exactly what she was doing.

"Look, Lib, I love you, but you drag me all the way out here to the middle of nowhere to, what, sit around all day? If I'm gonna be surrounded by nothing but cows, I might as well find myself a cowboy to shag."

And she *was* in the middle of nowhere. Woodvalley Pines, Wyoming was a long way from her home in Brighton, England. This hadn't exactly been what she imagined when she'd thought about moving back to America. The last time she was here, she'd been living in San Francisco, where she'd first met Libby. And she had to admit she missed the city. The hustle and bustle. Nights out. Takeout whenever you wanted it. The most exciting thing that had happened since moving to Woodvalley was the day Mrs Tucker lost her cat. For an hour.

"A dating profile full of innuendos is not gonna find you a cowboy. It's gonna find you a horny psychopath." Libby obviously wasn't done yet.

"You're being dramatic."

"Cat, at one point you wrote: *Before I take a long ride, I like to make sure my stud has had a good twenty minute warm up.*" Her best friend's eyebrow was raised, causing her to look all accusatory.

"What?" Cat not-so-innocently lifted her bare shoulder in a shrug. "That's just good horsemanship, Lib. You don't want him to be too stiff." She added a wink specifically to get a laugh out of her. And it worked.

Baked

When danger comes to the small town of Woodvalley Pines, Hunter vows to become the protector of local bakery owner, Rachel. But when things heat up, can this firefighter handle the burn?

Rachel was finally happy. She had a place to call home, amazing friends, and a successful bakery. Then her past found her. Now Hunter Campbell was in her kitchen, acting like a caveman. After months of only grunting at her, one little incident, and he has the audacity to tell her she's not allowed out without him. She couldn't decide what terrified her more about her new bodyguard – the giant hulk scaring off her customers, or the fire in her belly that made her heart race every time he was near.

Local firefighter Hunter was a man of few words. But if ever there was a time to talk, it was now. Rachel was in danger and there was no way he was going to let anything happen to his stubborn little fairy. It didn't matter that he'd spent months keeping his distance. Or that she had the power to shatter his heart and then stab him to death with the shards. This was happening. She could bang as many baking pans as she liked. He wasn't going anywhere. She was stuck with him.

Fighting fires was nothing new to Rachel or Hunter, but surrendering to the heat of the flames was a battle neither of them were prepared for.

Isobel Reed's stories delight and bring laughter to romance through sizzling dialogue and fast-paced writing. Fans of Hot Stuff by Carly Phillips or Rescue Me by Susan May Warren will love this sassy tale of a caveman fireman and the baker who wins his heart.

EXCERPT:

Striding down the terracotta cobbles like a man on a mission, Hunter knew what most people saw as they crossed the street to avoid him. But just because most people compared his physical build to the Hulk, it didn't mean he also had the whole wrath thing going on too. Although, if he was ever going to suddenly develop anger issues, this week would have done it.

He was pissed as hell. Nine months he'd stayed away. Kept his distance. Damn well tortured himself. And all for nothing. Because now? Now he didn't have a choice. There would be no staying away anymore. Not while Rachel was in danger. It changed everything.

What kind of man would he be if he let something happen to the woman he'd not been able to stop thinking about since he first laid eyes on her, just because he couldn't get over himself?

A shit one.

Exactly. He was fine being many things. A man of few words. A man most people had to stretch their necks to see fully. He was even fine being a man who tipped the loneliness scale a bit too enthusiastically. But he drew the line at being a shit one.

That being said, he knew what going to her meant. He wasn't dense. There had been a reason he'd stayed away. A good one. And now he was willingly throwing himself into the fire.

It meant he was done running. Done fighting his feelings. It was time to claim his honeybun. It was time to claim Rachel. And that's exactly what he was on his way to do.

Stopping outside the pastel pink storefront, his eyes went to the even pinker neon sign that hung above the window display. The name Fairy Baked was flashing above a line of pretty cupcakes that had been sprinkled with assorted candy.

You've got this. Just go inside and calmly explain that starting from today, she is not to go anywhere without an escort.

Easy.

Hothead

When a sexy fireman and a sassy filmmaker's worlds collide, can they stand still long enough to let love ignite, or will their instinct to run keep them from the one thing worth fighting for?

Luke Cappelli is the ultimate bachelor. He's never stuck around longer than one night, and no woman has ever tempted him to. *Until Bella.* With a face that rivaled an angel's and a mouth that could make a sinner blush, it was like she was created especially for him. Which is why committing to a few weeks of fun felt easy. But when it came time for her to leave, Luke realized letting her go wasn't just hard—it was impossible.

Bella had one job. Deliver a letter: that's it. Easy. She'd be in and out of Woodvalley Pines faster than you could say "howdy". Well, that was the plan anyway. Until she came face to face with broody firefighter, Luke Cappelli. With a sarcastic remark for every occasion and enough red flags to fill a parade, the man had heartbreaker written all over him. It didn't matter, though, because their time together had an expiry date, which was for the best. Wasn't it?

Fans of <u>Not the Marrying Kind</u> by Kathryn Nolan or <u>Hot in Here</u> by Sophie Renwick will be enthralled by Isobel Reed's sassy romances with witty dialogue and swoon-worthy happily-ever-afters. Grab a tall glass of water, find a cozy spot, and dive into HOTHEAD—a romance too sizzling to put down!

EXCERPT:

Collapsing into the bottom bunk, he let his head drop into his hands. Marco couldn't have been more than a few years older than him. Late thirties were no age to die. What the hell happened?

Maybe you should have read the letter and found out, dumbass. Or better yet, ask the fucking angel outside.

Speaking of. Just a second later, the door swung open, causing his head to shoot up.

Okay. Maybe she's not outside anymore.

"You always walk away from people mid-conversation, Luke ... or am I special?" she scolded.

She was special all right. "You always walk into rooms with big ass *Do Not Enter* signs on them ... or am I just lucky?"

A genuine sigh left those sweet red lips, enough to make him regret snapping back. "Look, I get this is hard for you. Believe it or not, I understand. My family are as dysfunctional as they come. Think the Lohans ... on meth. So, trust me, I get it."

Seriously, who the hell is this girl?

Rising from the bed, his feet were moving toward her before his brain had a chance to catch up. Only fully registering when nerve endings began lighting up as he sucked down more berries.

Before he knew it, he'd invaded her space. Personal bubble officially popped as his head bowed and their mouths lined up. All it would take was one small dip and he'd know for sure if those lips tasted as sweet as the woman who owned them smelled.

"Why are you here, Bella?"

He noticed her breath quicken. "Marco asked me to come." She rushed out. "To give you the letter and …"

"And what?"

"And h-he wanted me to stick around for a while."

He ignored the hammering of his heart at her declaration. His body couldn't be trusted.

"And why would he want you to stick around?"

"Are you going to take the letter?"

"You always answer questions with questions?"

Luke felt her breath warm his skin and found himself wishing away his stubble. He wanted to feel her sink into every inch of him.

Yeah. That's normal.

"Is this the proximity you conduct all your conversations?" was her reply.

It looked like he'd met a fellow smartass. The first one to drag a smile out of him.

This chick is something else.

Giddy-Up

Riley has spent a lifetime playing it safe, then she meets Wade—a cowboy who makes her want to play with fire. Will she finally find her voice and ask for what she's never dared to before, or will fear drive her to run once again?

Riley took growing up sheltered to a whole new level. She'd never so much as stepped out of Silver Valley. Now at thirty, she was taking the leap. In a new town. With a new job. And a new boss that made it hard to breathe, let alone use actual full sentences around. When hot cowboy, Wade Evans, flashed those dimples her way, she knew she was in trouble, she just had no idea how much.

Working seven days a week meant Wade didn't have much time for a social life. Let alone a love life. Not that he didn't want one. He did. Badly. So when Riley, the new maid, shows up, he doesn't shy away from making his interest known after it's made clear she feels it too. There's only one problem though, she keeps running from him. And he has no idea why. Now he has to decide whether to cut his losses, or fight for the one woman he's been waiting all his life for.

Fans of heart-stopping cowboy romances like <u>Wild Cowboy Ways</u> by Carolyn Brown or <u>A Cowboy to Remember</u> by Rebekah Weatherspoon will find the same exciting happily ever after in <u>Giddy-Up</u> by Isobel Reed. This best-selling author is known for her sarcastic dialogue and small towns filled with sassy characters. Saddle Up for a wild ride!

EXCERPT

Riley actually gulped. What on earth was Wade Evans doing here? Outside her staff-issued trailer, flashing those goddamn dimples at her and turning her mind to mush.

Like it wasn't mush before he showed up.

Okay. Fine. So it was plenty mushy already. It had been ever since yesterday afternoon when she'd been strong-armed into attending Zach's wedding. Zach was the oldest of the four Evans brothers. But he didn't work on the ranch like the others. Wade did though. He also just so happened to be the second oldest brother and the man in charge around here. And Riley's brand spanking new boss.

Where the hell is Bella?

That was a good question. Bella was the woman Riley had met yesterday and was responsible for the forementioned strong-arming. Where was she? She hadn't signed up to be harassed by dimples.

"Did you hear me, darlin'?" Wade drawled, this time tipping up his cream Stetson with one finger. "Bella's running late, so you're gonna have to make do with me as your escort."

Oh, she'd heard him alright. Hence the near catastrophic throb in her ears. This was the problem with social anxiety, how was she supposed to tell people she had it if her mouth was too dry to make sounds? It also didn't help that Wade of all people stood there. Staring. It was difficult enough to talk to regular people, but put a six-foot two, hard-bodied, blue-eyed cowboy in front of her and there was a strong possibility she may never speak again.

"Riley?" he prompted.

Say something. Anything.

"B-But…"

For the love of God.

This didn't bode well for the rest of the day.

AVAILABLE IN EBOOK AND PRINT WHERE BOOKS ARE SOLD

ABOUT THE AUTHOR

Isobel was born and raised in London. While she's a city girl at heart, she loves daydreaming about running away to a charming small town—though she's not entirely sure her husband and son would share her enthusiasm for the move. When she's not writing small-town romantic comedies or growing unhealthily attached to the characters in her books, you can find her reading, chasing after her very active toddler, or attempting to channel her inner domestic goddess in the kitchen (with varying degrees of success).

Known for her witty dialogue and swoon-worthy small-town heroes, Isobel signed with Inkspell Publishing in 2021. The following year, she released Love Tools, the first book in her four-book Bluestone Series. In early 2024, she launched Toasted, the debut novel of her seven-book Love Burns Series, which will roll out over the next year.

https://www.tiktok.com/@isobelreedbooks
https://www.facebook.com/isobelreedbooks
https://www.instagram.com/isobelreedbooks/
https://www.isobelreed.net/
https://www.amazon.com/author/isobelreed
https://www.goodreads.com/Isobel_Reed
https://www.bookbub.com/authors/isobel-reed